JASPER'S RUNAWAY BRIDE

MARGERY SCOTT

CLOVER RIDGE PRESS

JASPER'S RUNAWAY BRIDE

Copyright © 2018 by Margery Scott

All rights reserved

eBook ISBN: 978-1-988191-16-4

Print ISBN: 978-1-988191-42-3

MAIL-ORDER BRIDES OF SAPPHIRE SPRINGS

Miranda
Audra
Kathryn
Elise
Laura
Cassie

BRIDES OF COLDWATER CREEK

Josie
Sally
Anna
Beth
Willa

OTHER HISTORICAL ROMANCES

Emma's Wish
Wild Wyoming Wind
Rose: Bride of Colorado

MEDICAL ROMANCES

The Surgeon's Homecoming
Stranded with the Surgeon
The Firefighter and the Lady Doc

ROMANTIC SUSPENSE

A Time for Secrets
No One to Tell
The Stranger She Knows
A Question of Guilt

CHAPTER 1

"Y ou *will* marry Hubert, and I don't want to hear another word about it. He's a good match for you, and we all know there aren't any other suitors lining up to ask for your hand in marriage."

Lynna Spiers smoothed a fold in the French lace veil draped across her four-poster bed and raised her head to meet her mother's stern expression. "But Mama … he's so old … and he's so …"

Hubert Deline was at least in his late forties, more than twice her age. And twice her size, she added to herself. It wouldn't do to mention the size of the man's belly and his already fleshy jowls. Her mother would point out how shallow she was. She'd remind her that the man was a wealthy landowner who'd chosen her to be his wife and that she should be grateful she wouldn't be a spinster for the rest of her life.

She should be, she supposed, but after what her mother had told her the night before about marriage … and what happened on the wedding night … the thought of him kissing her, touching her …

She shuddered.

"What's wrong with you?" Her mother's brow creased in a frown. "Are you sick?"

Lynna shook her head. She was sick, but not in the way her mother thought. She felt physically ill at the thought of sharing Hubert's bed.

Did it make her vain that she wanted to marry a man who was reasonably physically fit, not repulsively obese? Whose lips didn't remind her of a fish? Not that he'd ever kissed her or that she'd had much personal experience with fish, but whenever he spoke, a vision of a fish she'd once seen gasping for breath, its lips flapping, popped into her head.

"Personally," her mother went on, "I'm surprised he wants to marry you since you have no dowry to speak of. Why, you know he's been very generous with our family since your nuptials were arranged."

This was the first Lynna had heard of his 'generosity'. What did that mean exactly? She had noticed changes for the better around their home lately, but was that due to Hubert's money? Had he basically … bought her?

Her mother let out a frustrated sigh. "Now stop being so foolish and finish dressing. Hubert is waiting in the garden to accompany you to the church. You have thirty minutes. Do not be late. The guests are waiting."

Her mother spun around on her heel and marched out. The door closed softly behind her, but to Lynna, it might as well have been a prison door clanging shut.

Marriage to Hubert Deline would be a life sentence of misery, and quite possibly, abuse. He'd already been married twice. His first wife had "gone to visit family" one night and had never returned. A short time later, he'd supposedly received a telegram that she had become ill and passed away. Lynna remembered his second wife, too, always with a fearful expression on her face. Lynna had often suspected there were bruises beneath the high collars and long sleeves the woman wore even in the heat of the summer. Then one day, she'd had an 'accident' and died, but because of his wealth and status in the community, it had never been investigated by the local constabulary.

Lynna slowly made her way to the window, the soft silk of her wedding gown swishing on the polished floor. With one finger, she nudged the curtain back and looked down onto the garden.

She'd always loved the view from her bedroom window at this time of year – the large manicured lawn, the abundance of flowers in full bloom and the perfumed air, and the wrought iron chairs and small table where she'd often sat, dreaming of her future.

Now, her future had been decided by her parents and Hubert. She would be Hubert's chattel, his property, to do with as he pleased.

A cold chill washed over her. What would happen to her when he tired of her?

She caught sight of Hubert standing with her parents near the fountain in the center of the stone path leading to the front door. He was nodding at something her father was saying, and her mother was smiling.

She glanced at the clock on the bureau. She was running out of time.

Her throat tightened and her heart began to race. It was difficult to even draw a breath. Her vision began to swim, and she held onto the edge of the bureau to prevent herself from falling. She recognized the sensations surging through her. She'd suffered from the same symptoms several times when she'd been in Hubert's company. He called it 'her delicate constitution' but she knew it for what it was. Panic!

She couldn't marry him.

She just couldn't.

She'd never once disobeyed her parents – at least not that they were aware of. She had had a rebellious streak, but she'd kept it well hidden. They'd always dominated her, told her what to eat, what to wear, how to act. And she'd always allowed them to control every aspect of her life – at least most of the time. She'd never even argued back. But now …

If she was old enough to be a married woman, to

manage a household and to be a mother within the next year or two, surely she was old enough to make her own decisions. Wasn't she?

And the first adult decision she was going to make was to run.

Now.

She doubted Hubert would be hurt, but he would certainly be furious. As for her parents, she'd miss them dreadfully, and they would be humiliated, but hopefully, one day they'd find it in their hearts to forgive her.

She had to leave before it was too late. She had no choice.

She didn't have time to pack a valise or to even change her clothes. If she wasn't downstairs within the next few minutes, her mother would come looking for her.

She had to be far away by the time they discovered she was gone.

Silver City, Colorado

Jasper Morrison nursed a cup of coffee in his sister, Deirdre's, kitchen. The room was small, but bright and airy. A soft breeze carrying the perfume of the lilacs lining the side of the house drifted inside.

"The meeting at the bank in Denver went well," he told her. "The note is paid and the manager told me they'd be happy to give me another loan if I need it."

"That's good news," Deirdre said, "but I don't understand why you didn't just go to the bank in Rocky Ridge."

"It's too small. It didn't have enough cash for me to do the expansion I wanted to do and to buy as much stock as I wanted to increase my herd. Denver really was the best option."

"So you added more outbuildings?"

He nodded. "Another stable and barn, and bought another five hundred head of cattle. And I've still got enough money to make the repairs to the house and add on the extra rooms."

Deirdre picked up a sugar cookie and nibbled on the edge. "The ranch is really growing. I won't recognize it next time I visit."

"It has changed since you were there last. It's been quite a while."

"It's just a shame you don't have anyone to share it with," she muttered, hiding her face behind her own coffee cup. "

His brows arched. "Excuse me?"

"You're building a legacy, but what's the point? Why are you working so hard? You're going to grow old in that big house all alone. And who's going to carry on once you're gone? You have no wife, no children to leave it to."

That was true, but that was going to change. Until a few weeks ago, he hadn't had time to think about getting married or having a family. He'd been busy. Every waking minute had been taken up with building the ranch. A year ago, he'd realized it had gotten too big for him to handle it all himself. He'd had to hire a dozen hands, then a foreman to oversee them so he could deal with the business of running the ranch and leaving most of the day-to-day chores to them. He still liked working with his hands, though, so he made time to do some of the chores himself.

"As a matter of fact, I have some news," he said.

Deirdre's eyes widened. "Don't tell me you got married and didn't tell me. If you did, I swear I'll—"

"I didn't, so don't get yourself in a twist. But I did go to the new matrimonial agency in Rocky Ridge and send away for a mail-order bride from back east."

Deirdre's voice rose and her eyes widened to saucer-size. "You what? Why in Heaven's name would you do that? What's wrong with finding a woman the normal way? Surely there are some desperate women in town who'd marry you? You're not *that* bad looking, and even though you're pretty stuffy and—"

"Thanks." He rolled his eyes and grinned at his sister, fully aware she was teasing him. "There isn't anyone in town I want to marry, so this was the next best thing."

"But marrying a stranger … that's such a gamble …"

"It is, but it can't be any worse than marrying a woman I already know I don't like, can it?"

"I suppose not …" She drew out the words. "Has this mail-order woman agreed to marry you?"

Jasper shook his head. "Not yet. We've been corresponding for a few weeks now. I've written a letter asking her to come west to marry me but I haven't mailed it yet."

"What's stopping you?"

"Nothing." That wasn't exactly true. He'd written the letter, but something had stopped him going to the railway depot in Silver City and buying a ticket for her trip west.

Deirdre set her mug on the table, leaned back in the chair and folded her hands in her lap. "Well, to be honest, I'm not sure I like the idea, but I do want you to be settled with a wife and a family, and if this woman will make you happy, then I approve."

She grinned. They both knew he didn't need her approval.

"Thanks. And I promise," he went on, "I won't get married without inviting you to the wedding."

"Good. Now, I need to get Jeremy up from his nap and take a package to put on the train. It will be here in an hour."

Jasper drained his coffee and got up. "How big is the package?"

Deirdre crossed the room to a counter running the length of the room and came back a few seconds later with a small box. "This is it. Why?"

"Let Jeremy sleep. I'll take it to the station for you. It's small enough that I can carry it while I ride, and I have to get back to Rocky Ridge anyway. As it is, I'm later than I figured so if I don't leave soon, I won't get home before dark."

Ten minutes later, after saying his goodbyes along with a promise to let her know if his mail-order bride accepted his proposal, Jasper mounted Fortune, his chestnut gelding, and made his way toward the train station.

Jasper had never been on a train, never even been close to one, but it seemed like an exciting way to travel. Maybe one day, he'd take a trip to California and see the ocean. He'd never seen the desert he'd heard about, either. Or … anywhere.

But if he was being completely honest with himself, he really wasn't in any hurry to leave his ranch. He was content there … or as content as he would be once he had a wife and a family. He only hoped Edith would feel the same way.

He heard the train whistle in the distance as he tethered Fortune to a hitching post near a long wooden building that served as the railway depot.

The railroad had only come through Silver City since the year before, and already the population in town had more than doubled. He understood that it was progress, but he was glad he didn't live in a city. He was happy on his ranch outside Rocky Ridge, where everybody knew him, where neighbors were friendly and helpful, and the air was clean, not tainted with coal smoke and fumes.

The package Deirdre had given him was going to

Los Angeles. He had no idea how it would get there, but the balding man behind the counter didn't seem concerned. He'd taken it, checked the address and Jasper had counted out the shipping cost.

Once their transaction was complete, Jasper tucked the receipt into his shirt pocket and turned to leave. He paused near the doorway, and for a few seconds, he considered turning back and buying the train ticket for Edith to come to him.

"Something else I can do for you?" the station-master's voice called out from behind him.

He looked back, shook his head, and stepped outside . A warm breeze stirred the dust into small whirlwinds, and weeds and dry brush tumbled along the dirt beside the track as the train chugged into the station.

The whistle shrieked and the brakes squealed as it came to a stop.

Lynna was hungry. So hungry. And thirsty.

She opened the drawstrings of her blue silk reticule and reached inside, wrapping her fingers around the single coin she had left. She took it out and opened her hand to look at it. Not even enough to buy a cup of coffee.

She'd stolen a handful of bills from the hidden compartment in her father's writing desk to make her escape, but after three days on the train, she'd realized she hadn't taken enough. Of course, she hadn't known how far away Colorado was and how long it would take to get there. Now, her money was gone other than that one coin.

When she'd tiptoed into the study and slipped the money into the reticule, she'd been sure she'd have enough left over after her journey west to find a respectable place to live and employment.

She'd been so wrong.

She could have cashed in her train ticket and disembarked the train in one of the towns closer to Boston, but decided against it. She needed to get as far away as she could.

She had no doubt Hubert or one of his hired men would come after her, and if they didn't succeed he'd hire a detective to track her down. She'd humiliated him in front of his friends and business colleagues. He wasn't the type of man to stand for her betrayal, which was how he'd interpret her action, or to be swindled, which was how he would think of her parents. He'd seek revenge or restitution.

She only hoped she'd be able to run far enough that he wouldn't be able to find her and take her back. It also meant she couldn't trust anyone. Hubert wasn't above bribery to get what he wanted. She wouldn't even be surprised if he put out a reward for information on her whereabouts.

"Next stop is yours, ma'am."

Lynna looked up to see the kindly face of the train's conductor. "Thank you."

"You're looking a bit peaked, if you don't mind me saying so." He peered at her face. "You have somebody meeting you in Silver City?"

She almost told him the truth, but at the last moment, she pasted a smile on her face. "I'm a bit tired from the trip, but I'm fine. I have family waiting for me," she said. "I do thank you for your concern, though."

"We'll be pulling into the station in five minutes or so. Can I get your bags for you?"

"Oh … no … but thank you," she said. "I can handle them quite well myself." She couldn't tell him she had no bags, that she'd fled in only the clothes she was wearing and money she'd stolen.

The conductor touched his finger to the brim of his hat and walked away.

A few minutes later, the whistle blew and the wheels screeched to a stop in front of a weathered building unlike any she'd ever seen before.

She stood up, and a wave of dizziness washed over her. Her vision blurred. Gripping the back of her seat, she dropped back into the seat until it passed. This time, though, she knew it wasn't panic that had brought on her symptoms.

She had to get off the train. If she was still on board when the train left the station and the conductor returned, she'd be arrested since she didn't have a ticket. Then she'd be thrown in jail, which meant when Hubert caught up with her, she'd be trapped.

She couldn't let that happen. She'd have to force herself to put one foot in front of the other until she was on dry land. Then, she could sit somewhere until she felt stronger.

She'd learned that deep breaths helped, so she forced herself to calm down, and then she stood up again. This time, although she was still a little unsteady on her feet, she managed to make her way to the end of the car and step down onto the ground.

"Have a nice day, ma'am," the conductor said, then picked up the portable wooden step and set it down inside the train.

"Thank you," she muttered.

Looking around, she realized the station was empty. A bench rested against the wall of the depot, so she climbed the three steps and crossed the wide wooden porch and sat down, folding her hands in her lap and taking in her surroundings. Not nearly as large as Boston, the town of Silver City was set far enough away from the railroad tracks to avoid the smell of the burning coal that came from the trains but close enough for the townspeople and passengers to easily reach the depot even on foot.

The town was a mish-mash of buildings separated by a wide dirt street. Men on horseback rode down the street, while wagons rolled by, some parked in front of a large building she assumed was the mercantile.

Some of the buildings were brick, and some were painted, while others were nothing more than weathered wood shacks. A church stood at the opposite end of the town, it's steeple rising into the clear blue sky.

"All aboard!" the conductor shouted. Passengers leaving on the train hurried inside and a few minutes later, the train pulled away in a hiss of steam and a shriek of the whistle.

Lynna's stomach rumbled. Surely there was a café or diner in the town, she thought. She had no money to buy a meal, but at least someone might take pity on her and give her a glass of water.

She got up and took a few steps before the dizziness returned, Her vision clouded and she grew warm. Too warm.

She thought she heard a man's voice calling out, but she couldn't focus enough to know where it was coming from.

Blackness overcame her.

CHAPTER 2

Jasper saw the woman wobble, and he ran toward her as her legs gave out and she crumpled. He barely reached her in time to wrap his arms around her and break her fall before her head smashed against the side of an iron post.

Carefully, he lowered her to the floor. Her eyes were closed, her long dark lashes resting on her pale cheeks.

"Somebody help!" he shouted, hoping the stationmaster could hear him over the whistle still blowing, the shrill noise carrying on the summer air.

Moments later, the door opened and the stationmaster hurried out. "What's going on?"

"Go fetch the doctor."

The man didn't move. Instead, he hooked his thumbs in the waistband of his pants and stared down at the woman. "What's wrong with her?"

"I have no idea," Jasper snapped. "She needs a doctor."

"She got money?"

"What?"

"No point going to get him unless she does. He won't come."

Jasper couldn't believe the man would refuse to get help … that a doctor would refuse to treat a patient who couldn't afford to pay him. Rocky Ridge might be small and not have a train yet, but he'd bet Doc and Grace, the two doctors in town, would ever turn a patient away based on their ability to pay.

"She looks a bit tetched," the man said, his gaze lowering to the woman's clothes. "What kind of woman goes around in a get-up like that?"

Jasper hadn't even noticed what she was wearing, only that the skirt of her dress was smeared with dirt and what looked like grease. There was a long tear in one sleeve and bits of lace hung from the hem. Maybe she wasn't in her right mind, but he'd worry about her wardrobe later. Right now, she was unconscious.

Gently tapping the woman's cheeks, he spoke. "Ma'am? Can you hear me?"

Her lids fluttered, then opened. Her eyes widened in terror and she screamed, scrambling to get away from him and scraping her elbows in the process. "Get away from me," she cried out. "I'm not going back. Now or ever."

"Ma'am," he said quietly while he raised his

hands in surrender. "I'm not going to hurt you. You fainted."

She peered at him for what seemed like a full minute, her eyes narrowed, before she spoke again. "I fainted?"

He nodded.

"I need to get home," the stationmaster interrupted, then turned on his heel and locked the door to the depot behind him. With a last glance and a slight shake of his head, he walked away, disappearing around the side of the building.

"Where aren't you going back to?" he asked. "Are you in trouble?"

"No … yes … I need to go."

She struggled to sit up, then slumped back into his arms.

"Ma'am, you're ill, and you might be hurt." He thought he'd caught her in time to stop her injuring herself, but he wasn't sure. A person could be torn apart on the inside without it showing on the outside. He knew that from when his uncle had gotten thrown from his horse a few years back. "You need to see a doctor."

"No. I just need to get away …"

"From who? Is someone after you? Did someone hurt you?"

She shook her head, then grimaced. "I need to hide for a while, that's all. And I need … water … and food …"

Food? "You're hungry? When was the last time you ate?"

"I'm not sure," she croaked out. "Two days ago maybe? When we stopped for meals along the way, they wouldn't even give me water since I didn't buy food. Can you take me to your house?"

"My house?"

She nodded. "You have food at your house?"

"Well … yeah …"

"Please?"

She must be desperate to be willing to go off with a man she'd never met before where she'd be at his mercy. Whatever she was fleeing from must be even more terrifying than taking a chance with her modesty and possibly even her life. How could he not help a woman who was so afraid she'd take that kind of risk?

At the same time, he couldn't help being suspicious. Who was she running from? For all he knew, she'd escaped from a lunatic asylum somewhere and had stowed away on the train. Maybe the people she was fleeing from were chasing her to take her back to a padded cell where she belonged.

He'd always trusted his gut, though, and his gut was telling him she was as sane as he was, although right now, he wondered about his own mental state, taking a woman he'd never seen before home with him.

"I live a day's ride from here," he told her. "We wouldn't get there until tonight."

"That's even better," she said. "I can manage without food until tonight." Her gaze flitted around the depot.

Was she looking for whoever was after her? Or something else?

"Do you have a wagon?"

"No," he replied. "The trip would be a lot easier if I did. I have a horse, so you'll have to ride. Are you okay with that?"

The horrified expression that filled her face couldn't have been any worse if he'd asked her to stand buck naked in the middle of the street, but she didn't object. Instead, she tucked her legs under her and used his arm to hoist herself onto her feet. He reached out to steady her in case she fainted again, but she sucked in a breath and straightened to her full height, which barely reached his chin. Then she turned to him. "Can we go now … please?"

For the first time, he really looked at her. Dark brown hair shot through with reddish strands curled around her face, and he noticed a faint scar near her hairline. Her bluish-grey eyes glistened with unshed tears as she looked up at him.

His chest tightened and warmth seeped through his veins when he met her gaze. He'd heard that a man could be entranced by a woman, but he'd never thought it was really possible.

Until now.

Lynna's heart raced. As if running away from her own wedding wasn't bad enough, she'd practically thrown herself at a stranger and begged him to take her miles away from civilization. Why hadn't she thought about escaping sooner?

Because she'd foolishly believed her parents would relent at the last minute and not force her into a marriage she didn't want. She'd been wrong.

Fear snaked up her spine. Once they were out of Silver City, she'd be at his mercy. He could kill her. Or worse. Yet she didn't have any choice. This man had been the only one willing to help her, and if it came down to it, whatever he did to her couldn't be worse than what Hubert would do to her if she went home and married him.

"What's the matter?" The man's voice stole into her thoughts. "You're looking at me like I'm Satan."

She tried to laugh, but it came out as a brittle sound. "Are you?"

"Nope," he replied with a smile. "Haven't done any devilish deeds for at least a couple of days. So are you ready?"

She didn't answer immediately. This was her last chance. "Yes," she said finally. "Let's go."

He took her hand and tucked it under his elbow, then led her to the end of the platform and down the steps to the ground.

The dirt was uneven with hardened footprints. "Watch your step," he warned. "It's easy to turn your ankle when it's like this."

She lowered her gaze, focusing on where she was going. Thank goodness it's dry, she thought. It would be a river of mud if it was raining.

The man guided her around the side of the depot until he reached a huge tan-colored horse tethered to a hitching post. Then he released her and turned his attention to the horse. She listened as he spoke softly to the animal and ran his hand gently down its neck. The horse nickered as if it understood every word.

A faint smile tugged at her lips. A person could tell a lot about another person by the way they treated animals. This man would have his faults, she was sure, but she sensed he was basically a kind man, and the fear that had almost overwhelmed her only a few minutes before eased a little.

She was still on edge, and likely would be until they reached their destination, but for now, he seemed nice enough.

She didn't move as he unhooked a canteen and opened it, and then handed it to her. "Take small sips," he said, "or you'll be throwing it back up. It's full, and we can get more water on the way."

The water cooled her parched throat, and even though she was tempted to gulp the entire contents, she resisted. He'd been kind enough to help her. She wouldn't risk him changing his mind because she was being contrary.

"Do you know how to ride?" he asked.

"No." She took another small sip. "I never had any reason to. We used a carriage when we went out."

His gaze lowered to her gown, now streaked with grime. "I don't have a sidesaddle so you can either ride astride or walk."

She looked down at her shoes peeking out from under her gown. The satin brocade slippers on her feet were not meant for walking any distance, especially over uneven ground.

He followed her gaze, and her face flushed. Another few inches and he would have seen her ankles! "I'll try to ride," she murmured.

"Okay, but one more thing before we go," he said. "I don't usually travel with people I don't know, and you haven't even told me your name."

"Oh … you're right … I apologize … I'm Lynna Spiers of Boston, Massachusetts." She held out her hand.

The man wrapped his hand around hers, and her fingertips tingled. The sensation swept up her arm and through her body to her toes. So unusual, she thought.

"Jasper Morrison," he said, then added as an afterthought, "of Rocky Ridge, Colorado."

By noon, Lynna felt human again. The idea of sitting astride a giant beast while it moved under her had frightened her. She'd given herself a stern talking-to, reminding herself that she wasn't the browbeaten young woman who'd left Boston. She was a strong woman who'd taken her life into her own hands, and if she couldn't bring herself to do something she'd seen so many men do, she deserved nothing more than to be married to a man who'd domineer her.

Calling on every ounce of courage she possessed, she'd allowed Jasper to help her mount and situate herself on the saddle. Once she was settled, he'd taken the horse's reins and began walking slowly away from the depot.

She'd held on to a knob on the front of the saddle as if her life depended on it, but by the time they'd left Silver City behind and were on a narrow trail, she'd gotten used to the gentle sway of the horse under her as it moved and she'd been able to relax a little.

"You look more comfortable now," he commented once they'd been on the trail for a while.

She smiled. "I am. It's actually quite pleasant. I never thought I'd enjoy riding, but now I think I'd like to learn properly one day."

He drew the horse to a stop. Still holding the reins, he opened one of his saddle bags and took out an apple. Lynna's mouth watered.

"Here," he said, handing it to her. "I saw you're holding on with just one hand now, so I think you can eat something without falling off."

"Thank you." She took the apple and wiped it on one of the few spots on her gown that wasn't dirty, then took a small bite. "Apples are so much better here than in Boston," she gushed after taking a few dainty bites. "I've never eaten one that tasted so good."

"I think it's just because you're so hungry." He glanced up at the sky. "We'll stop for a rest and lunch in an hour or so. My sister packed enough food to feed us for a week."

Turning away, he flicked the reins and they began to move again. His hair, almost black, curled against the collar of his tan shirt. Broad shoulders tapered into the waistband of black pants, a gunbelt resting on his hips, the holster at his side.

"Your sister lives in Silver City?" she asked.

He nodded, his back still to her. "She moved there when she got married."

Conversation died, and they traveled in silence while Lynna finished her apple. Not knowing what to do with the core, she tucked it into the pocket in her gown. She smiled inwardly at the memory of her dressmaker's horrified reaction when Lynna had insisted on pockets in her wedding gown. Now she was thankful she'd been so stubborn.

As she rode, Lynna was enamored by the scenery. She'd never seen so much open space, such sky where the small puffy clouds seemed close enough to touch, so many wildflowers covering the land.

Mountains rose in the distance, the colors blending from green to shades of grey and purple, with white tips.

Enjoying the warmth on her skin and her surroundings, she didn't really notice the time passing until Jasper led the horse to a bend in a creek and stopped.

"We'll rest here," he said, looping the horse's reins around a tree branch. "I'll help you down."

He held out his arms and Lynna slid out of the saddle. His hands spanned her waist as she fell against him and he gently lowered her to the ground.

She'd never been that close to a man, and her breathing quickened. His scent, a unique smell she couldn't identify but that she found pleasant, wafted to her nose. She looked up at him, noticing for the first time the flecks of gold in his eyes and the tiny lines that fanned out from the corners. He must smile a lot, she thought.

Her heart tumbled inside her chest. Mercy, what was happening to her?

For a long second, neither of them moved, until suddenly, the sound of movement in the underbrush nearby startled her.

Her heart leapt into her throat and she pulled away, realizing she should have been mortified to have a man's hands on her waist, to be in such an intimate position with a man, especially one she barely knew. Yet she wasn't embarrassed at all. What did that say about her? Was she a harlot deep briside?

"Nothing to worry about," he assured her. "Likely a squirrel or a rabbit or something. If you need to take care of … anything … you could go over there." Jasper pointed to a stand of cedars nearby.

Now her cheeks flamed. She did need to take care

of personal business, but it wasn't proper to even suggest such a thing to someone else. Still, out here in the wilderness, if she suddenly disappeared behind a tree, it would be obvious what she was doing.

Things were definitely different here in the west, she mused as she made her way to the trees. There seemed to be no sense of propriety or privacy. Or maybe it was just him.

She'd have to wait until they reached his home and she spoke to more people to find out.

By the time she returned, Jasper had spread out fried chicken, bread and cheese, with cherry pound cake for dessert.

"I bet you're still pretty hungry," he said when she was standing beside him.

"I am." The apple had helped, but she was far from satisfied.

"You going to be able to sit down in that contraption?"

"Of course," she replied with a confidence she didn't feel. He looked on, a faint smile on his face, as she twisted and tucked and pulled at her gown's frothy layers of fabric, her petticoats and crinolines, not to mention the bustle and train on the back of her gown.

Finally, though, she was sitting beside him, her breathing heavy, the gown spread out around her. She couldn't prevent the chuckle that escaped her. "This really is a day for new experiences," she said. "I've never sat on grass before."

"Is that so?"

"Mama always said it wasn't proper."

"You'll find out here people do a lot of things that they don't think is civilized back east."

She nodded, eyeing a chicken drumstick.

"Go ahead," he told her. "You're going to have to eat with your fingers."

She was reluctant, but as he'd pointed out, she was in the west now. With a grin, she gingerly picked up the chicken and took a bite. It was delicious, better than many of the meals she'd eaten at some of the finest restaurants in Boston.

She ate silently until she was afraid if she ate more, she would be sick. "May I have more water, please?" she asked, then smiled. "I'd get it myself but …" She glanced at her skirts, and he laughed as he got up.

"Stay there!"

He came back a few moments later and handed her the canteen. "We'll fill it back up before we move on."

"Thank you."

He lowered himself to the ground and faced her squarely. "Now, want to tell me your story?"

"My story?"

"You're not from around here, your clothes look expensive and you're running away from something or somebody."

She put the cap back on the canteen and set it in her lap. "He'll send someone after me to take me back," she said when she was finished telling him the events that led to her arrival in Silver City and her fear that Hubert would punish her for humiliating him. "I have no doubt about that. It would be better if he came himself, because I'd recognize him and could avoid him, but he won't do that. He'll send one of his men instead."

"You'll be safe at my ranch," he said.

"I don't want to be obligated to anyone, so I need to find a way to support myself without taking charity. Since running away was a spur-of-the-moment decision, I didn't make plans. I could have saved more money and had a valise packed. I didn't even know where I was running to. When I got to the train station, I showed the ticket master how much money I could afford to spend on a ticket and asked him how far I could go. If I'd realized food was so expensive, I would have kept more money aside. As it was, I ran out."

"You got yourself into quite a predicament, didn't you?"

She nodded. "If you hadn't come along …" Her voice trailed off and she felt tears threaten.

"Well, I did, and you'll be safe now."

She wasn't convinced that was true, but she was safer than she'd have been if she'd stayed in Silver City. As long as she didn't put Jasper in danger, she'd figure out the rest once she got to Rocky Ridge.

"You finished eating? Need more water?" Jasper asked. If somebody really was after Lynna, they needed to stay on the move and not give her pursuer a chance to catch up.

She shook her head. "I've had more than enough, thanks."

"Then I'll fill the canteen and we'll head out. There's an abandoned cabin part way where we'll have to spend the night. As it is, if we don't get a move on, we still might not get there in time. It'll only take an hour or two in the morning to reach the ranch. A little longer if you want to go right into Rocky Ridge."

He held out his hand to help her up. Heat shot through him, settling low in his belly. He recognized the feeling.

Why wouldn't he be attracted to her? She was pretty, and he was sure once she was rested and cleaned up, she'd be downright beautiful.

He hadn't been with a woman in a long time. He'd been far too busy to think of those things, but now, with her standing so close …

A frown creased her forehead and a wariness filled her eyes. "Back in Silver City you said we'd reach your ranch tonight."

Her soft voice interrupted his wayward thoughts. Good thing, too. He was going to marry Edith. "That's if we were both riding," he told her. "Walking is going to slow us down."

"Could we get there tonight if we both rode?"

"Well … yeah, probably, but …" He stopped talking, his gaze shifting to the back of her gown. "That thing takes up more saddle than I do." He'd never been able to understand why women wore so many petticoats and padded their backsides. What was the purpose? It was as if they were trying to disguise the fact they had backsides, but instead, the padding only drew men's attention to that part of their bodies. Made no sense at all, but then there was a lot of things about women he didn't understand.

"You mean you've walked all morning because of this?" she asked, splaying her fingers on her bustle.

"There wasn't room for you, me and that," he answered. "I'll just fill the canteen and then we'll move out."

He turned his back to her and wandered down to the bank of the river. He crouched at the edge and dipped the canteen into the cool water, his thoughts on the woman waiting behind him.

Was he making a mistake taking her with him? He was busier than usual now that he'd increased his herd and he still had to finish the addition to the house. He didn't have time to play nursemaid or to entertain.

He'd offered, though, so he had no choice but to take her home with him now. She'd said she didn't want to be obligated, but once she was rested, he could offer her some money to help her out, take her back to Silver City and put her on a train to wherever she wanted to go.

Yet even though the decision made sense, something about it bothered him. She'd be alone, with no one to protect her if her fiancé did come after her.

No, he realized, he couldn't send her away. Not knowing what happened to her would bother him too much. He had no choice but to let her stay at the ranch until the threat – if there was one – was over.

The decision made, he capped the filled canteen, got up and climbed back up the riverbank.

Lynna was gone!

CHAPTER 3

"*L*ynna!"

Lynna heard him call her name just as she was adjusting the skirt of her gown. He sounded angry, although why he would be, she couldn't imagine. What had she done?

"Lynna! Where the hell are you?"

"I'm here," she called out as she stepped out from behind the trees and carefully picked her way down the slight rise toward the riverbank. Her wedding slippers were definitely not suitable for walking on uneven ground.

She closed the gap between them, meeting his gaze. Was that concern she saw in his eyes? "What's wrong?"

"It's not smart to go wandering off out here," he pointed out. "Once you're in the trees, you can lose your bearings real quick and get lost. What were you doing in there, anyway? I thought you'd already … you know …"

His sharp tone rankled Lynna. Did he really think she was so foolish? "Believe it or not, I am smart enough to stay close by. I had … things … to take care of." Her cheeks heated, which infuriated her even more.

A sense of satisfaction tweaked her when she noticed a faint flush to his face as well. She hoped he was embarrassed that he'd brought up such a personal subject again.

"Sorry …" he muttered, turning away to hang the canteen strap on the saddle horn then tightened the cinch around the horse's belly.

"You ready …?" His voice trailed off as he studied her and lines appeared between his brows.

She smiled at him. "Something wrong?" she asked sweetly.

"Something's different," he said. Then his eyes widened. "You got rid of your …" He pointed his finger in the general direction of her bottom.

"Bustle," she finished for him. "And yes, I did. And the crinolines and the petticoats. I had no idea you'd walked all morning because of it. I've never seen two people ride the same horse before, so I thought you were being chivalrous and letting me ride. I didn't realize two could ride the same horse."

"It's not very comfortable and it's not real good for the horse, but two people will fit on a saddle."

That didn't seem possible, but if her bustle was

the reason he'd been walking, then she'd leave it behind. "Now you can ride, too."

"What about your things? Where are they?"

"Behind the trees," she replied. "They're too bulky to carry."

"You sure you want to leave them behind?"

"I'm sure."

"Then let's go," he said.

Lynna put her foot in the stirrup and wrapped her hands around the saddle horn. With an unladylike grunt, she used every bit of her strength to hoist herself up and swing one leg over the saddle the way Jasper had shown her that morning. The leather felt cold on her bare skin. She couldn't remember anything other than a warm washcloth ever touching her inner thighs.

"You okay?" Jasper asked.

She nodded, and a few moments later, he swung himself into the saddle behind her. His muscled chest rubbed against her back, and even through the silk of her gown, his heat warmed her.

Mercy! She'd never expected him to be *this* close to her while they rode. That kind of intimacy was highly improper, especially with a stranger. According to her mother, even allowing her husband to touch her outside the marriage bed was improper. Yet here she was, allowing this man she barely knew to not only touch her back, but to practically glue himself to her.

She straightened, doing her best to keep her body

away from his as his arms wrapped around her to take the reins and set off.

It wasn't long before her back muscles ached from holding her posture so rigid to stay away from him. She soon realized avoiding him completely wasn't even possible. Finally, she couldn't hold her position a moment longer. Her body sagged against him.

He shifted behind her, and his body seemed to cradle her. Proper or not, it felt … nice. The slow steady rhythm of the horse's movements and the sense of comfort she felt surrounding her lulled her into a state of semi-sleep. Suddenly, in her mind she saw herself resting against Hubert's chest. She let out a gasp at the horror of it.

Jasper tugged on the reins and the horse stopped short. "What's the matter?"

She looked over her shoulder to see concern etched on his face. She let out a soft laugh. "Nothing at all," she said. "I …" How could she explain that she'd found herself actually enjoying his closeness until her vision of Hubert? "I'm fine."

He nodded, and they moved on again.

"Tell me about Rocky Ridge and your ranch," she said a while later. She really wanted to ask if he was married and had children, but questioning him would be rude. Besides, surely he couldn't have a wife waiting for him. Could he?

Not that she cared. She wouldn't be at his ranch any longer than necessary. As soon as she found some employment and saved enough money, she'd buy another train ticket to … somewhere. Somewhere far away.

"Not much to tell," he began. "I grew up in Rocky Ridge on the ranch, me, my folks and my sister. When my folks passed on, it came to me. I bought up more land and cattle. I added another wing to the house a little while back, but it's pretty much the same as it's always been."

"How far from town is the ranch?" She hoped it was close enough that she would be able to get to town every day for work until she'd saved enough money to leave.

"About three miles," he replied.

"I see." That was quite a distance for someone who wasn't used to walking more than from the front door of her house to a waiting carriage. Still, she was determined she'd be independent so she'd have to get used to it.

The afternoon wore on. The pale blue of the sky deepened and the sun disappeared behind the mountains in the distance, casting a golden glow along the peaks.

She shifted so she could look at him over her shoulder. "Do you think we'll reach your ranch tonight?" she asked as the trail gradually descended into a valley. "Daylight is fading fast."

He nodded. "That's Rocky Ridge," he said, gesturing with his head toward a faint shadowy outline in the distance. She never would have been able to identify them as buildings if he hadn't told her. "We don't have to go all the way to town. We should make it to the ranch before it gets pitch black, but even if we don't, we won't have far to go in the dark. The sky is clear so the moon will give us enough light. Mrs. Platt will have supper waiting, too, I'm sure. I don't know about you, but I could use a decent meal."

Lynna was so exhausted she wasn't sure she'd have the strength to lift a fork to her mouth, but she wouldn't refuse his hospitality. "Mrs. Platt?"

"She's my housekeeper but she's really more like family. I don't remember a time she wasn't here," he replied. "From rapping my knuckles when I tried to steal a cookie right before supper to helping me to bed when I got drunk after my folks got killed, she's been right there through everything. I stay out of her way and let her run the house the way she's been doing as far back as I remember, and she takes care of me the way she always has."

"It sounds as if you're very fond of her."

"I am."

"That's so different from the way I grew up," she said. "We had a succession of housekeepers while I was growing up until recently. To be honest, I doubt my mother even knew their names. It's unusual that yours stayed so long, and that you're so fond of her."

"You'll find a lot different here from back east."

"I already have," she commented.

It seemed night fell more quickly in Colorado than it had in Boston, but she wasn't sure if it was her imagination. The stars felt closer, too, almost as if she could reach up and touch them.

Within minutes, the sun had disappeared. Luckily, the moon was almost full and helped to light their way.

Being alone with Jasper in the moonlight seemed so … intimate. She supposed she should be a little afraid. After all, she was alone with a stranger in the dark. Yet she had no fear at all. In fact, she felt a sense of closeness that was unexplainable.

She couldn't help wondering if he felt the same way. And she also couldn't help wondering why she hoped he did.

Lynna opened her eyes the next morning to sunlight streaming through the window. For a few seconds, it didn't register in her brain that this wasn't her bedroom in Boston. Then her gaze settled on a wooden dresser with a jug and basin on top and a straight-backed chair beside it. Then everything came back to her.

She'd been barely able to walk by the time Jasper had helped her dismount when they'd finally reached the ranch house.

In the darkness, she couldn't see the details of the house, only that it was large and had a wraparound porch. He'd ushered her into the house and into the kitchen where he'd introduced her to Mrs. Platt, who'd sat her down to a bowl of chicken and dumplings at the kitchen table. As soon as she'd finished eating, she'd been shepherded up the stairs by Mrs. Platt, given a nightgown to change into and had been tucked into bed as if she were an injured child. She'd fallen asleep almost immediately and slept soundly, waking only once when she'd heard a rooster crowing. It had startled her for a few seconds, then she'd snuggled back under the blanket and gone back to sleep.

She looked around the room, at the canopied bed covered with a pale blue flowered quilt and the lace curtains at the window. A woman's room. Since it didn't seem likely this would be Mrs. Platt's room, she assumed it had once been Jasper's sister's bedroom.

She was about to get out of bed when she heard a faint knock at the door and it opened before she had a chance to respond.

Mrs. Platt bustled in, her wrinkled face creased in a smile and her eyes sparkling with merriment. "Well, then, you look a might better than you did last night," she said. She crossed the room and picked up a jar of salve she'd left on the nightstand the evening before. "Did the salve help?"

"It did," Lynna replied. "How did you know I'd need it?"

Mrs. Platt chuckled, the lines in her face deepening. "I'm not so old that I don't remember how the insides of my legs felt the first few times I was on a horse. I suspected yours might be a bit tender after riding all day."

"They were. Thank you."

"Most likely you'll be a bit stiff for a day or two as well," Mrs. Platt went on as she crossed to a wardrobe in the corner of the room and opened the door. "When you feel up to getting out of bed, you can try on one of Deirdre's dresses. Deirdre is Jasper's sister, if he didn't tell you that. She left some of her things here when she moved to Silver City. There's petticoats here, too, if you've a mind to wear them. Some folks wouldn't want to wear somebody else's underthings, but they've been boiled, so they're clean. But it's up to you."

"Oh, I couldn't wear her clothes ..." Lynna protested.

"You planning to wear that wedding dress until it falls off you, are you?"

The woman was right. Her gown was filthy and torn. If she ever planned to go into town and find employment, she'd have to at least look respectable.

So much for her plan to be independent. She'd already had to rely on Jasper for food, shelter, transportation and clothing. What else could she possibly be indebted to him for?

Mrs. Platt's voice interrupted Lynna's thoughts. "Breakfast will ready in a few minutes," she said. "I'll bring you up a tray."

"Oh ... no ..." Lynna sat up, and swung her legs out of the bed, swallowing down a moan as the muscles she'd never used until the day before protested. "That's not necessary. Thank you for the clothes. I'll dress and come right down."

"Are you sure? You're still looking a bit under the weather."

"I'm sure. I feel much better this morning. You and Jasper have done enough already. I don't want to impose more than I already have."

"It's no bother," Mrs. Platt said. "I'll see you downstairs then." She turned and left, closing the door behind her.

Doing her best to ignore her aches and pains, she quickly got out of bed and looked through the dresses in the wardrobe. They were plain and practical, but well-made. She chose a pale yellow cotton dress with a white frill around the hem.

After a few minutes, she gave up trying to tie herself into her corsets and slipped into the dress. She finger-combed her hair and pinned it into a loose knot at the nape of her neck, and after giving herself a last look in the mirror, she ventured downstairs.

She'd never been seen by anyone other than her mother and the housekeeper without being properly groomed, but now she had no choice. She couldn't hide in the bedroom forever, and at least she wasn't outside where anyone else could see her. And with any luck, Jasper would be out doing whatever ranch people did.

Unfortunately, luck wasn't with her. Jasper was sitting at the kitchen table poring over a newspaper when she walked in. "Good morning," she said, suddenly feeling shy.

Jasper looked up and smiled. "Morning," he said. "You sleep okay?"

"I did, thank you."

"Sit yourself down and eat," Mrs. Platt interrupted, tapping the back of a chair facing Jasper.

Lynna did as she was told, and seconds later, a plate heaped with ham, eggs and potatoes appeared in front of her.

"There's more if you want it," Mrs. Platt told her, bustling around the kitchen and setting a mug of coffee in front of her and then refilling Jasper's mug before she left the room.

Jasper folded the newspaper and set it beside him on the table. "You look better than you did last night."

Lynna's cheeks burned. "I feel much better, thank you," she said, lowering her head to stab a piece of fried potato with her fork. "If you could point me in the direction of town, I'm going to see if I can find some work."

"Work?"

She nodded. "You sound surprised. I am capable of earning a living." She just hadn't figured out how yet.

He pushed his plate back and leaned his elbows on the table. "It's not that. I just figured it would take you a few days to get back on your feet first."

"While I appreciate your generosity, I don't want to impose on you any longer than I have to. I need work so I can find somewhere to live while I save enough money to move on."

"I see." He took a sip of his coffee, his gaze never leaving her face. "And what kind of work are you planning to get? Do you have any skills to get a job?"

"Well …" There was the fly in the ointment. She didn't.

"Can you cook?" he asked.

"I watched our housekeeper cook, but I've never tried it myself. It doesn't look difficult."

"Keep house?"

She shook her head.

"Teach school?"

Even though she could read, write and do sums, she wasn't a qualified teacher. She shook her head. Her employment options were quickly disappearing.

"What can you do?" he asked.

She tore her eyes away from his, her gaze flitting around the kitchen as if she'd find an answer in the pie safe or on the shelves. "I … I'm excellent at embroidery and petitpoint," she told him.

"I've heard of embroidery but I'm not sure even what it is," he said. "The only kind of stitching I know about is what makes shirts and pants. Can you do that?"

She shook her head. Her family had always had a dressmaker to sew their clothes until recently. She hadn't had anything new since her father had fallen on hard times. Until recently. She sucked in a short gasp as the realization hit her – the new dresses her mother had had made for her had been paid for with Hubert's money.

"What else?"

Dragging her thoughts back to her present predicament, she frowned. She had to think for long seconds. There was very little of a practical nature that she was proficient at. As a girl, her mother had assured her she'd never need the basic skills it seemed she'd need to be able to support herself.

"I … I'm quite good at playing the harp." As soon as the words left her mouth, she regretted them. The harp? Really? From what she'd seen of the west so far, there wouldn't be much call for a harpist.

Just as she feared, her comment brought about a burst of laughter from Jasper, his booming voice filling the kitchen. "Sorry," he said. "I shouldn't have laughed, but I doubt you'll find a harp within a hundred miles of here."

"I suppose you're right."

Her heart sank. With no skills, what were her chances of finding employment, especially in a small town where she knew no one?

She couldn't go back to Boston, though. She just couldn't.

He got up, picked up his mug and took it to the counter that stretched the length of the kitchen. He slid it into a basin filled with soapy water and wiped his wet hands on his pants. "I'm going into town tomorrow," he said. "Let me talk to some people and see if I can find somebody who'll give you a chance to prove yourself."

After he left, Lynna sat at the table nursing her coffee for a while, her gaze focused on the black liquid in the cup. What was she going to do?

Jasper really was one of the kindest men she'd ever met, so unlike any of the men she knew in Boston.

She hadn't seen any sign of a wife or children the night before. Was he married? And even more so, why did she care?

CHAPTER 4

Jasper drew the wagon to a stop in front of Todd's Mercantile the next morning and climbed down. He'd promised Lynna he'd try to find someone who'd hire her, even though he'd been pretty sure it would be a fool's errand.

The aroma of coffee beans and spices met his nose when he opened the door. Elias's daughter, Camelia, was behind the counter. She looked up and smiled at him as he crossed toward her, his boots clicking on the wooden floor. He took off his hat and ran his fingers through his hair. "Morning, Cammie," he said. "Is your pa around?"

Cammie shook her head. "He's upstairs in bed. Got a touch of gout, I think, but the stubborn man won't let the doc take a look at him."

"I see." Since Elias dealt with most of the folks in town regularly, Jasper had figured he'd be the best one to ask. Now, he wasn't sure where to try next.

"Anything I can do for you?" Cammie's voice burst into his thoughts.

"Well … there's a young woman at my ranch who needs work. I was hoping your pa might know of somebody who's looking for help."

"The Patterson's housekeeper just left to go back to Missouri," she told him. "Maybe—"

"She's not a housekeeper."

"What does she do?"

He let out a short chuckle. "That's the thing. She doesn't know how to do much that's of any use out here. She's from back east and it sounds like she grew up never having to learn anything practical."

"Hmm …" Cammie shook her head. "That is a problem. I can't think of anybody who'd take a chance on her. Except the Pleasure Palace, that is."

Jasper nodded absently. It had crossed his mind as he'd driven into town that Bryce Malton, the owner of the Pleasure Palace would be happy to hire Lynna – a beautiful and innocent woman who would end up just like the other soiled doves who entertained the cowboys who rode into town on Saturday nights for money.

His chest tightened at the thought of men kissing her, touching her, doing things … He wouldn't think about that, because he wouldn't let that happen. He wouldn't allow anyone to destroy her, which was what would happen within weeks if Malton got his hands on her.

"Just thought I'd ask," he said to Cammie as he

put his hat back on. "I'd appreciate it if you'd keep your ears open and let me know if you hear of anything. And give your pa my regards."

"Will do, Jasper," Cammie replied.

His other errands completed an hour later, Jasper headed out of town toward the ranch. He'd gone half way when he remembered the letter in his pocket. He'd meant to mail it to Edith while he was in town, and he'd completely forgotten about it.

That was the second time he hadn't sent the letter. What did it mean? Surely a marriage proposal was important enough that if he really wanted Edith to come west to be his wife, he wouldn't have forgotten to mail the letter.

Maybe he didn't really want a wife. Or maybe … just maybe … Lynna was taking his mind off marrying a woman he didn't even know. Maybe somewhere deep inside his mind, he was thinking about marriage to the woman he'd met only one day before but who already stirred something inside of him he'd thought was long dead.

All during the drive back to the ranch, thoughts swirled in his head. It was the perfect solution. He would have the wife he wanted, and Lynna would have the financial security she needed, without having to resort to working at the saloon.

Lynna didn't get a chance to speak to Jasper when he got back from town. She'd looked out the window when she heard someone approaching and she'd seen him drive the wagon past the ranch house and stop at the barn.

She'd waited, but when he came out of the barn, he'd been on horseback and had ridden away.

It was after supper that evening that he asked her to join him on the front porch. Her stomach fluttered in anticipation. Surely he must have found someone in town who was willing to hire her.

Night had fallen, the blistering heat of the day gone and replaced by a soft breeze rustling in the trees nearby, and the moon was hidden behind the clouds in the sky.

She perched on the edge of a rocking chair while he leaned against the porch railings, facing her.

"I'm sorry," Jasper said when he'd finished telling her about his conversation with Cammie. "She said she'd let me know if she hears anything."

The sympathy in Jasper's voice almost undid her, but she blinked back the tears threatening to fall and swallowed the lump forming in her throat. Crying wouldn't solve her problem.

She wanted to be independent, but without some way to support herself, that independence would never come. "Thank you for trying," she said softly.

They sat in silence for a long moment. Crickets chirped. Somewhere in the distance, a coyote let out a howl.

"What will you do?" he asked finally.

She shook her head, even though she knew he couldn't see her. She couldn't take advantage of Jasper's hospitality indefinitely, and without work, there was only one thing she could do. She'd have to go home.

Nausea roiled in her stomach at the thought of what awaited her back in Boston – the disgrace, Hubert, her parents.

No, she couldn't face them all. And worse, even if they forgave her, she couldn't face marriage to Hubert. Why, she'd rather work in a brothel … Well, she wouldn't, but she couldn't think of anything worse than letting Hubert touch her and … do things to her.

Much as she hated to be indebted to anyone, she could ask Jasper to lend her the fare to move on and get settled, and then repay him. Her heart sank. It was her only option, unless something totally unexpected happened.

Pasting a smile on her lips that belied the desperation and fear she held inside, she answered in as cheerful a tone as she could muster. "When one door closes, another opens. I'm sure something wonderful is just around the corner."

Jasper looked out the window and sighed. It had been raining steadily for almost two days, and still there wasn't even a glimpse of blue in the sky. How much longer was this weather going to go on? He had work to do, and the longer the rain lasted, the longer it would take to round up the cattle when it stopped. It never failed that when they had a heavy rainfall, some of the cattle got mired up in mud and he and the hands would have to ride the whole ranch to find them and then spend hours getting them out.

He turned at the sound of light footsteps behind him and saw Lynna coming into the room. She walked with grace and elegance, the skirt of the pale blue dress she was wearing softly swaying with each step. Deirdre's dresses were a little snug on Lynna, but they only emphasized the curves he couldn't help noticing. Curves that sent lustful thoughts surging through his brain and causing reactions low in his body.

She was a beautiful, desirable woman, and over the few days she'd spent here at the ranch, he realized he was growing to care about her more than just a house guest.

"Looks like this rain is going to last for a while," he said as she came to stand beside him at the window. "But even when it's gloomy outside, I love the view."

"It is very pretty," she agreed. "So different from my view back east."

"Does it rain much in Boston?" he asked.

She nodded. "I didn't mind, though. I kept busy until the skies cleared and I could go outside again."

"So you never had to work?"

"No. Once I was finished with my education, I stayed at home. My father didn't believe women should work."

"Did you get much schooling?" he asked.

"More than most girls, I imagine. My father believed I should be able to converse on any subject."

"You talk like one of the teachers I had growing up."

Lynna's brows arched. She gazed up at him as if she wasn't quite sure whether his comment was an insult or a compliment. "Oh? How did your teacher talk?"

"Proper. You can tell when you talk that you've had schooling. So maybe you could teach school somewhere out here where they don't need a real one."

Lynna shook her head. "I'm not a teacher, only an avid reader. I wanted to apply to the medical college in Boston and become a physician. There were only a few females who had ever been admitted, but I wanted to try. My father wouldn't hear of it."

"Why not?"

"He felt it wasn't proper for a woman to study the human body." She chuckled. "He also thought it was a waste of time since I'd likely be married and my husband wouldn't allow me to work. He didn't know I'd planned to leave Boston as soon as I graduated and go to Canada."

"You didn't think of coming west?"

She shook her head. "No, I didn't. I'd heard of

Emily Stowe, who had a medical practice in Toronto, and I'd hoped to go there and work with her." She sighed. "But it wasn't to be, so I did the best I could. I convinced a friend – a male friend – to go to the medical college and buy the books. I hid them in my bedroom and read them cover to cover. I couldn't learn any practical techniques, but I did study anatomy and physiology and learned about medicines and surgical techniques in the books."

"Without your parents' knowledge?"

She nodded, a slow smile creasing her lips. "In their presence, I read, sewed, played games."

"What kind of games?"

"Chess. Backgammon. Cards." She giggled, the soft sound sending a tingle through Jasper's veins. "But most of all, if my parents were out, I played billiards. My father would have had apoplexy if he'd caught me, but he never did."

The woman played billiards! The more he learned about Lynna, the more Jasper admired her. She was no wilting violet. Impulsive, obviously, but definitely not afraid to go after what she wanted. He liked that. It was rare to find that quality in a woman, but he had to admit it attracted him.

"Now, if you'll excuse me, Mrs. Platt is going to teach me how to make biscuits."

"What … oh … sure … If you have time later, maybe we can have a game of backgammon."

Lynna gave him a wide smile, and his insides quivered. "I'd like that, but I warn you, I'm quite competitive."

She turned her back on him and crossed the room. He watched her go, and an unexpected sensation of contentment washed over him. He could see himself spending his evenings with her, talking, playing a game or two, holding her, kissing her …

He wouldn't let his mind go there, not while he couldn't get down to the river to take an icy bath.

His thoughts strayed to Edith, the woman he'd been planning to marry until Lynna had dropped into his life.

Would he feel that way about her? Would he want her the way he wanted Lynna? And it wasn't just physical desire either. He knew that, even though Lynna was penetrating his dreams during the night as well as distracting him from his chores during the day.

It was more than that. From what he'd read in Edith's letters, she was pliable and yielding, agreeing with whatever Jasper suggested. While that kind of personality would make life simple, he wondered if it would eventually be dull. Edith had no opinions of her own. Until recently, he'd thought he wanted that kind of woman.

Now he wondered. Did he really want that kind of relationship?

"Let the competition begin," he said to the empty room, a smile tugging at his lips and anticipation growing inside him.

The rain stopped during the night, and by morning, the sun was shining and it was warm enough to spend time outdoors. When Jasper mentioned he had some supplies to order at the mercantile in town, she couldn't resist asking if he'd mind if she went with him.

She didn't *have* to go into town, but she'd found the evening before that she enjoyed his company. Over the backgammon board, she'd discovered he was a good conversationalist, with informed opinions on many topics, but at the same time he'd been willing to listen to hers, even if she'd disagreed with him. Which she had, often.

They'd talked late into the night, and had only said goodnight when she'd found her eyelids closing and he'd caught her trying to stifle a yawn.

As she lay in bed later, she'd admitted to herself that she would miss him when she left. But she had no choice. She couldn't accept his hospitality indefinitely

"Are you sure you aren't too tired today to make the trip into town?" he asked over a breakfast of sausages and eggs they were sharing at the kitchen table.

"Not at all," she assured him. She was exhausted but she had an errand in town she was anxious to deal with. Once she took care of that, she'd know better what she needed to do to leave.

"Then I'll meet you out at the wagon in a half hour."

The trip into Rocky Ridge was much too short. The sun glistened on the still-damp leaves, birds soared overhead, and a soft cedar-scented breeze filled the air. Their conversation was light and she enjoyed his dry sense of humor.

"I'll see you back here in an hour," he said when he drew the wagon to a stop in front of the mercantile.

An hour was more than enough time for what she had to do, so she nodded and allowed him to help her down out of the wagon. She noticed his hands rested on her waist a few seconds longer than they needed to, and she also noticed she enjoyed the warmth that seeped through her thin cotton dress.

Leaving her on the boardwalk, he opened the mercantile door and stepped inside. She walked a few yards, then when she was confident he wouldn't come back out and see where she was going, she hurried toward the Wells Fargo office they'd passed on their way into town.

A small balding man with a pair of spectacles perched on the end of his nose glanced up from a newspaper when she opened the door, the bell tinkling to announce her arrival.

"What can I do for you?"

"Does the stage go to Denver?" she asked.

The man nodded. "Tuesdays and Fridays."

"What's the fare? One way."

"Depends," he replied.

By the time she left the office a few minutes later, her mind was spinning. She'd had no idea the fare depended on whether she had luggage, whether she was willing to sit beside other travelers or if she needed a seat alone.

It didn't really matter, she mused, her spirits sinking. She wouldn't be able to afford even the cheapest fare for quite some time. Unless … She could ask Jasper for a loan. Just enough to pay her way to Denver and rent a room in a boarding house long enough that she could find some employment. She may not have many skills, but surely she could find a position in a shop, or even a … factory.

Surely he'd be happy to lend her the money to get her out of his house. She wasn't going to ask him to give it to her as a gift. She fully intended to pay him back as soon as possible.

Still, she wasn't sure she'd have the gall to ask.

As she tried to decide her best course of action, she strolled down the boardwalk toward the mercantile. Several ladies nodded their heads in greeting as she passed, and she returned their smiles.

In a way, it was a shame she was leaving. She could make friends here. She was sure of it. But she had to leave.

Enjoying the sunshine, her thoughts drifted to

Jasper, as they usually did these days. It was hard to keep her mind off him. She missed him when he was out on the range, and she found herself looking forward to seeing him in the evenings.

She felt her lips twitch in the beginnings of a smile, her gaze drifting down the street. People hurried about, intent on their own errands. Wagons rolled down the street, and her gaze landed on a scrawny tortoiseshell cat sitting beside the livery stable licking its paws.

Her gaze drifted to a man riding into town on horseback. She looked on as he drew on the reins and slid off the saddle when the horse slowed to a stop beside a hitching post.

The rider looped the reins around the post and made his way toward the door of the livery

Although he was too far away for her to recognize the man's features, something in the way the man moved stirred a memory in Lynna's brain.

Her heartbeat tripped. Her breath caught in her throat and she felt the blood turn to ice.

CHAPTER 5

"Morning, ma'am," Jasper touched the brim of his hat as he held the mercantile door open for an elderly woman to pass.

The woman nodded an acknowledgement. Then Jasper went inside and greeted Elias Todd behind the counter. "Morning, Elias," he said, taking off his hat and scrubbing at his hair. "Any mail for the ranch this week?"

Elias walked the length of the counter to a desk and stand of mail slots. He reached into one of the slots and drew out an envelope. A tiny smile creased his lips when he handed it to Jasper and gave him a knowing glance. "It's from your ladyfriend."

It made sense that Elias would recognize Edith's handwriting since she'd sent Jasper several letters, but it still made him uncomfortable that Elias knew about their relationship. And if Elias knew, so did everybody else in town.

Jasper's insides clenched as he plucked the letter from Elias's hand. He should be pleased to hear from Edith. So why did he feel … indifferent, as if a letter from her was nothing more than a note from an acquaintance? He felt a little guilty that this was the third time she'd written to him since the last letter he'd sent.

He wasn't being fair to her. He knew that. Edith had made it very clear that she'd welcome a marriage proposal and she was more than willing to travel to Colorado.

Until Lynna's arrival, he'd been settled about his intentions toward Edith, too. But something had changed, and even though Lynna had made it very clear she'd be leaving as soon as possible, and she had no intention of getting married, he couldn't get her out of his mind.

He tucked the envelope into the pocket of his pants. He'd read it later. And he'd make up his mind what he was going to do once and for all.

Bart Abrahams! Lynna was sure of it! Hubert had sent Bart after her. His face was shadowed by the Stetson on his head and the glare of the sun, but she recognized the way he stood, his knees locked, his hand resting on the butt of the gun in the holster at his side, the way he swaggered into the livery stable a few seconds later.

She had to hide. If he saw her …

She bounded up, her knees trembling. Lifting her skirt a few inches, she hurried down the boardwalk steps to the ground and raced into the narrow alley beside the mercantile. She slipped into the shaded space, her back glued to the wall. She forced a few deep breaths into her lungs.

After a minute or two, she slid her back along the wall until she could peek out and see the livery stable. Her throat was parched and tight, and she swallowed thickly against the fear pounding through her veins.

Two women approached, giving her a curious glance as they passed by, their heads together. No doubt they were gossiping about the strange woman in the alley.

She couldn't worry about that now. She had to keep her wits about her. Taking a quick glance toward the back of the alley, she felt a little better. If Hubert's henchman came in her direction, she'd slip out the back and escape into the trees.

Suddenly, a shadowy form filled the opening. She tried to scream, but the sound froze in her throat.

A fraction of a second later, a voice – a familiar, soothing voice – penetrated the terror overwhelming her.

"Lynna! It's me!"

It took a few seconds for Lynna's brain to register the man's face. Jasper!

Jasper was reaching for her. Tears of relief blurred her vision and she fell into his arms, her fingers clutching his shirt. His arms wrapped around her and pulled her into his chest as he eased her out of the alley into the sunshine.

For long moments, she didn't move, just reveled in his arms around her, calming her fear.

"What happened?" he asked once she'd stopped shaking and she'd loosened her hold on him. "Why were you in the alley?"

"He's here," she croaked past her parched throat. "Bart's here."

"Who?"

"Bart! Hubert's right-hand man! He's here."

Jasper's head flitted from side to side as he searched both ends of the street for someone he didn't recognize. "Where?"

She squinted into the sunshine, her eyes targeted on the far the end of the street. "In there," she said, pointing toward the livery stable. "I saw him … he went into the livery … I'm sure it's him. Oh, Jasper, I knew he'd find me. I have to hide—"

She tried to pull herself out of Jasper's grasp, but he held firm, drawing her back into the circle of his arms. She gave up and burrowed her head into his chest.

"It's okay," he said quietly. "You don't have to go anywhere. I'll keep you safe."

She wanted to believe him, but her mind wouldn't let her. She shook her head, her tears dampening his shirt. "No, I have to—"

Gripping her shoulders, he pushed her away from

him and hooked his finger under her chin. Gently, he raised her face. "Look at me!"

When she met his gaze, his dark eyes bored into hers. "You're safe. I won't let anyone hurt you. I promise. If it'll make you feel better, I'll go over to the livery now and take care of it. What did he look like?"

"Tall. Thin. A brown shirt. Two guns. If it is him … there was a rumor that he'd killed a man in cold blood because the man spilled a drink on him. They couldn't prove it, though, because nobody would testify—"

"Nobody's going to kill me," he assured her. "Now stay here and let me go check."

Lynna wrapped her arms around her waist against the sudden chill inside, but she nodded and watched Jasper walk away toward the livery.

If anything happened to Jasper … Her breathing hitched. She couldn't bear it if she was the cause of Jasper being hurt, or … No, she wouldn't even let the word form in her mind.

As she looked on, Jasper strode down the street and disappeared inside the livery stable, returning a minute or so later. "The man you saw was Toby Arnprior," he told her when he stopped beside her. "I've known him for years."

"What?" How could that be?

"I checked with Landry Mitchell. He's owns the livery stable. The only person who's been there all morning is Toby. That's who you saw, not somebody your fiancé sent to find you."

Relief warred with embarrassment, causing Lynna's cheeks to burn. "I was so sure …" she murmured.

"At that distance, he probably looked like the man you thought he was. But it wasn't. Now if you're ready, let's go home."

She stood for a moment, her heart accepting that she'd let her imagination run away with her. She'd allowed her fear to overrule reason, and because of that, Jasper had risked his life for her.

Because if it had been Bart, it was quite possible Jasper could have been killed.

She was still convinced that one day soon, either Hubert or one of his men would track her down. And Jasper, being the honorable man he was, would try to protect her.

He could die because of her.

She couldn't let that happen.

The ride home was quiet. She slid a glance at Jasper. Sunlight glistened off the golden strands in his dark brown hair, and she noticed a shadow of stubble on his chin. Instead of making him look unkempt, it made him even more handsome.

She couldn't help wondering how that stubble would feel against her skin. Would it burn? Be painful? Or would it create sensations that would be exciting?

She'd never know, because there wasn't time. She had to leave Rocky Ridge as soon as possible before Hubert or one of his men found her.

Today, she'd made a mistake, but she was convinced that next time or the time after that, she wouldn't be wrong. And when that day came, Jasper would be willing to die to protect her.

She knew one thing – she would never go back to Boston. She would fight whoever tried to force her until her last breath. She'd rather die than ever see Hubert again.

Especially now. Now that she'd met a man like Jasper. Until now, she'd never known men like him existed, and as much as she was fighting against it, she felt herself becoming more and more attracted to him with each passing day.

And because she liked him, respected him and was developing more feelings for him than she'd ever thought she was capable of, she knew she had to leave before it was too late. She would never be able to live with herself if something happened to him because of her.

Was what she was feeling love? Or was it merely concern for another's well-being? She wasn't sure. She only knew that Jasper's safety was more important to her than her own happiness.

"A penny for your thoughts."

Jasper's voice interrupted her musings. "Still thinking about what happened?"

"No," she lied. Well, it wasn't exactly a lie. The

incident in town was what prompted her thoughts of escape … and her feelings for Jasper … but she wasn't thinking about the man she'd mistaken for Bart.

"You're awful quiet," he pointed out.

She forced a smile to her lips and instilled a lightness to her voice. "Just planning my strategy for our next backgammon game."

He laughed then, the tiny creases beside his eyes deepening and the sound of his laughter filling the silence. Oh, how she loved the sound of his laughter.

But she had no choice. After supper, she'd speak to him and ask for his help to leave.

Something was wrong with Lynna! She'd been terrified when she'd thought one of her fiancé's men had tracked her down. That made perfect sense, from what she'd told him about the man her parents had tried to force her to marry.

But she'd been wrong. She was safe. So why was she still so tense, so quiet on the ride back to the ranch? When he'd asked her about her thoughts, she'd tried to convince him she was plotting a game-winning strategy. She'd avoided his gaze, but her smile was tense and didn't reach her eyes, and while she tried to sound cheerful, there was a quiver in her voice that gave her away.

Supper had been strained, and when he'd

ventured outside to take care of a few chores after the meal, she'd seemed relieved to see him go.

He was still pondering it when he crossed the yard toward the house and found Lynna sitting on the front porch. Her head was lowered, and she was twirling a strand of hair around one finger.

As he climbed the steps, she looked up, startled. Hadn't she heard him coming?

"Did you take care of your errands in town today?"

She nodded. She'd only had one goal, and that was to find out the fare to Denver and then the train fare to California. The stage fare to Denver was expensive, but the train fare to Los Angeles, the largest city she could think of and therefore the safest place to disappear, was exorbitant. Which was why she'd realized it would take far too long to save the money herself, even if she could find work. She had no choice but to lower her pride.

"Ready to do battle over the backgammon board?" he asked with a grin as he stopped and leaned his hip against the railing in front of her.

"Maybe later …" she replied absently. She got up, but didn't make a move to go inside. "There's something I need to talk to you about first."

"What's that?"

"I appreciate everything you've done for me, but I can't stay here indefinitely."

She could, he wanted to contradict. He'd grown used to her being here, and if he was being completely honest, she'd filled his house with something he'd never thought he'd find. He couldn't define it, only knew that if she left, she'd take it with her and his life would be as empty as his house.

"So, I'd like to ask one more favor."

"Name it."

"I need a loan, enough money to get far away from here. California, maybe. And enough to pay for a room somewhere and food until I find a job. In a city, I'm sure I could find work in a shop somewhere."

"Lynna," he began.

She rested her hand on his arm, sending heat flowing through his veins.

"I'll pay you back. I promise. With interest. I'm an honest person, and—"

"I'm not worried about you paying me back."

"So you'll lend me the money?"

"I can't." He could afford to lend her enough to support her for a year or two, but he wouldn't. The truth of the matter was that he couldn't stand the thought of her leaving, of not knowing where she was, if she was safe. Heading west wasn't an easy trip, and for a woman, it was rife with danger. She'd been lucky she'd made it to Colorado without being robbed, or worse. His conscience wouldn't let him help her to put herself in that kind of danger again.

Even more surprising to him, though, was the fact that he'd started looking forward to coming home to her in the evenings. There was no question she was nice to look at, and his body reacted to her more than it had to any other woman he'd ever known.

If he could convince her she was safe in Rocky Ridge – with him - maybe, just maybe they could build on that.

But if that happened, it would create another problem. What to do about Edith.

Edith was expecting a proposal. He knew that. And until a few days ago – until Lynna – he'd been ready to ask her to come west and be his wife.

The letter he'd written asking her to marry him was still in his pocket, along with the letter he'd picked up in town earlier. He hadn't been able to bring himself to mail his letter to Edith, and he wasn't in any hurry to read what she'd written to him.

He should be. He knew that. The fact that he wasn't eager to read what his future bride had written to him was a sign as sure as if he'd been smacked with a hammer.

"I'm sorry, Lynna," he said softly, "but no."

The hope he'd seen shining in her eyes died and her whole body seemed to slump. "I see."

"I would give you the money if it was for anything else, but not this. It's not safe——" He started to explain why he wouldn't give her the loan, but she interrupted him before he could finish.

"You don't have to justify your decision."

He took a few steps toward her. "You know you're welcome to stay as long as you want to."

She raised her head to look him squarely in the

eye. "And do what? As long as I'm in this town, I can't support myself, so how will I ever be able to save enough to move on?"

She did have a point, but Jasper still couldn't give in, knowing that by lending her the money she'd asked for, he'd be putting her life in danger.

"Maybe Mrs. Platt could teach you how to cook and keep house and you could find a job as a house-keeper," he suggested. "Maybe you could qualify to become a schoolteacher. Or—"

"While I live under your roof and accept your charity."

"It's not like that," he countered.

"That's exactly what it's like." She smiled sweetly, but he couldn't help be hear the steel in her voice. She spun around and headed toward the door. She stopped her hand on the handle and turned her head back to face him. "This isn't your problem, and I apologize for making it yours. I'll think of another way." A few seconds later, the door slammed behind her.

CHAPTER 6

Lynna pulled back the curtain the next afternoon and looked outside in time to see Jasper riding away. Although he was on horseback, it looked like he was heading in the direction of Rocky Ridge. Strange, she thought. He usually took the wagon when he went into town.

Her temper flared again. He could have offered to take her with him so she could try again to find work since he wouldn't help her. Instead, he'd gone off alone, virtually holding her prisoner at the ranch.

Now she was being dramatic, she scolded herself. She was far from being held hostage. She was just piqued at the situation she was in.

She hadn't seen Jasper since she'd stormed inside the night before. She regretted her minor tantrum. She should never have let her temper get the best of her, but what right did he have to dictate what she could and couldn't do? He wasn't her father or her husband, and those were the only two men who had any authority over her.

"Lunch will be ready in an hour," Mrs. Platt said as she came into the parlor, a dustrag in her hand.

"Thank you, but I won't be here for lunch," she replied. "I'm going into town." She'd find work, one way or the other. If she had to, she'd have to force herself to go and see the owner at the Pleasure Palace. Jasper had assured her she could find work there. At the time he'd mentioned it, she'd sworn she'd never lower herself to that level. Never say never, she thought.

"That's three miles," Mrs. Platt pointed out. "Are you sure you're up to walking that far, especially in those shoes?"

Lynna's gaze followed Mrs. Platt's down to the satin slippers – her wedding slippers – she had on her feet. A three-mile walk wouldn't be pleasant, but she had no other shoes, and none of the shoes Deirdre had left behind fit her.

"I have no choice," she said. "I need work, and one way or the other, I'm going to find it. I may have to do something I don't want to do, but whatever it takes to earn a living, I'll have to do it."

Mrs. Platt opened her mouth as if she was going to say something, but then closed it, shook her head and continued her dusting.

Lynna left the room and went upstairs to fetch her hat and reticule. She gazed at herself in the mirror for a few moments. She'd changed since the day she ran away. Gone were the ringlets and curls she always wore, as well as the sparkle in her eyes. Lace and silk had been replaced by serviceable cotton and muslin. Gone was her old life, and as much as a new life was what she wanted, she did miss much of it.

Pitying herself wasn't going to help, she chided herself. She had to find a way to earn money, one way or the other. And the sooner she got started, the sooner she could leave.

Jasper dismounted and tied his horse to the hitching post outside the sheriff's office in Rocky Ridge. His meeting with the bank manager had lasted longer than he'd expected, but he'd been satisfied with how it went by the time he left.

The sun rode high in the sky, and he took off his hat and ran his shirt sleeve across his forehead. He paused on the boardwalk for a few seconds before he went into the sheriff's office, raising his hand in greeting to two men loading a wagon in front of the mercantile. Friends, neighbors, people he'd seen in and around town moving about, taking care of their own business. A normal morning in town.

He opened the door and stepped inside. The aroma of coffee brewing on the pot-bellied stove in the corner of the office met his nose. Zane Morgan, Rocky Ridge's sheriff, was leaning back in a chair, his feet resting on the desk, his ankles crossed. He looked up from the book he was reading as Jasper closed the door behind him.

"Morning, Jasper," Zane said, lowering his feet to the floor and putting the book on the desk. "Haven't seen you for a while. How are things at the ranch? Everything okay?"

Jasper nodded. "I guess you heard I've got a woman living at the ranch right now."

"I did hear something about it," Zane said, getting up and indicating a chair on the other side of the desk. "Sit down. Coffee?"

"Wouldn't mind one, thanks."

While Zane poured black coffee into two metal mugs, Jasper told him about Lynna and the reason he was there. "Have you seen any strangers around lately?" he asked Zane when he was finished.

Zane handed him a mug. "Can't say I have," he said as he sat back down behind the desk. "A few cowboys came into town Saturday night, but they're long gone by now. I'll keep an eye out for anybody that looks suspicious or comes around asking questions and let you know."

"Thanks."

"I know what it's like for a woman to live in fear. After what Priscilla and I went through with her husband ..." He let the sentence die out.

He didn't need to go on. Jasper, as well as everybody in town and the surrounding area, knew what had happened between Zane's wife and her first husband. It had been a terrifying time for them both, but it had ended well and now they were happy.

The conversation turned to general news, and by the time Jasper had drained his coffee, an hour had passed. He got up. "I'd better be going," he said. "Still have a lot to do this afternoon." He held out his hand to Zane. "Thanks."

Zane shook his outstretched hand. "Glad to help if I can. I'll let you know if I see or hear anything."

Jasper nodded an acknowledgement and left the office. He trusted Zane to do what he could, and by the time he reached the ranch, he was anxious to talk to Lynna and assure her she'd be safe.

"Mr. Carstairs, I'm sure I could wait tables just as well as Mrs. Carstairs if you just give me a chance—"

The café owner shook his head, but not before his gaze raked over her. "I'm sure you could, and I'd bet the customers would like looking at you while they took their meals, but I can't come up with one good reason why I should pay you to do something my wife does for free."

Lynna's gaze strayed to the owner's wife watching them with narrowed eyes through the opening between the kitchen and the eating area. The woman was painfully thin and haggard, and since Lynna knew she had five children to care for as well, it was no wonder she was exhausted. "Your wife could likely use some help—".

"Don't you worry about my wife. She's just fine."

"But—"

"Unless you're going to order something, I'd best get back to work." He turned his back on Lynna and walked away.

Lynna sighed and left the café, dropping onto a bench in the shade of the barber shop a few feet away. She'd spoken to every shop and business owner on the street, and not one of them had offered her a position.

Well, that wasn't exactly true. She would have been hired in the gunsmith's shop if she'd known how to repair firearms. She'd been tempted to lie, but since she'd never even handled a gun, she was afraid she'd pick one up and shoot herself.

At least Claire Morgan, the owner of The Lucky Shamrock Saloon, had been sympathetic to her situation, but sympathy didn't earn her any money. She'd wished she could help, but she'd just hired a barmaid the month before and couldn't afford to hire another.

There was only one place she hadn't gone to – The Pleasure Palace. Could she really do it? Could she let men … She didn't really know what men did with women, but whatever it was, men were happy to pay them, and the women who worked there seemed to invite their attention. Perhaps it wasn't as bad as she'd been led to believe.

Getting up, she trudged toward the large two-story house near the edge of town. The closer she got, the more her stomach quivered so much she was growing nauseated.

As she neared the house, she noticed two women standing on the second-floor veranda. One was dark-haired and was wearing a frothy yellow dressing gown that was open in front for everyone to see. Under the dressing gown, the woman's voluptuous breasts spilled out over her corset she didn't even try to hide. The other woman was smaller, but dressed in a similar fashion.

As Lynna stopped on the street in front of the house, the second woman crossed to rest her hands on the railing and look down at her. "You looking for Bryce, or just gawking?"

"I … I guess I'd like to speak to the owner."

The first woman joined her friend. "Looking for work?"

Was she? Could she bring herself to flaunt her body the way these women did? She took in a deep calming breath, tempted to turn and run as fast as she could back to the ranch, but that wouldn't help her at all.

She'd been mistaken about the man she'd thought was Hubert's henchman, but she was convinced Hubert or one of his men would come after her. With his connections, it wouldn't be hard for Hubert to find out which train she'd taken and where she'd gotten off.

She couldn't stay in Rocky Ridge, even though she wished she could. She'd be happy living at the ranch with Jasper for the rest of her life, but that wasn't possible.

If she ever wanted to get out of Rocky Ridge and escape Hubert, she had no choice. She needed money, and this was the only way to earn it. "I am," she replied with much more bravado than she felt.

The two women laughed. "I hope you don't think you're going to make much money dressed like that, honey," the first woman continued. "Men don't want women who look like their wives or one of them nuns that come around sometimes."

"I—"

"There's enough business to go around," she went on, "so we'll help you once Bryce hires you on. Just go on inside. You'll find him in the parlor."

"Thank you," Lynna croaked. Her knees shook and her heart beat like a hummingbird's wings as she climbed the steps to the front door.

"Lynna!" Jasper called out when he went into the house after rubbing Fortune down and giving him water. "Where are you?"

Mrs. Platt appeared at the doorway to the kitchen, a rolling pin in her flour-covered hand. "She's not here."

Jasper frowned. "Where is she?"

"She went to town," Mrs. Platt told him. "I've been worried sick since she left."

"Town?

Mrs. Platt nodded. "Went off not long after you did."

"Why didn't she ask me to take her?" In the time she'd been at the ranch, she'd never left the house unless he was with her.

"Said she was going to find work, one way or another," Mrs. Platt told him. "I have a feeling she'll end up at the Pleasure Palace if she can't find anything else."

Jasper's insides lurched and his throat tightened. He'd already spoken to everyone he could think of to find work for her, and had failed.

Maybe she'd be able to win one of the merchants over with her poise and her fresh beauty. He hoped she could, because if she didn't, Mrs. Platt might be right. She might end up going to see Bryce Malton, the owner of the Pleasure Palace.

Malton was lower than a snake. He'd made a fortune from the women who sold their bodies in the bedrooms of the whorehouse.

Most of the women who worked there had had no other choice, and Malton took advantage of their desperation. Jasper had heard about what Malton did to those women before he let customers have their way with them. One woman a few years back hadn't survived to earn her first dollar.

Jasper's chest squeezed so tight it was hard to draw a breath. His stomach clenched and his heartbeat tripled.

"If Malton lays one hand on Lynna," Jasper said, even though Mrs. Platt had already gone back to rolling out her dough, "I'll kill him with my bare hands."

Even as the words left his mouth, Jasper was shocked at the fury in his voice. But he meant every word.

"I'll be back later," he called out to Mrs. Platt. "I'm going to find her." And hope I'm not too late, he added to himself as he raced to the barn to saddle his horse again.

He would feel the same no matter what woman it was, he tried to convince himself as he urged Fortune along the trail toward Rocky Ridge. No, he amended. While he sympathized with the women who found themselves so desperate they'd sell their bodies to men, how he felt about Lynna was different.

Because … the realization hit him like a punch to the gut. He was falling in love with her. He'd been attracted to her that first day and wanted her like a man wants a woman, but he'd had no feelings for her. Since then, though, her vulnerability, her sweetness and her strength had attracted something deep inside him.

Usually Jasper enjoyed the ride into town and used the time to work out problems or just to enjoy the fields of wildflowers and high grasses, the scent of pine and cedar carrying on the warm breeze. Not today.

He'd almost reached Rocky Ridge when he

rounded a bend in the trail and caught sight of Lynna sitting in the grass at the base of a tree, her back against the trunk, her arms wrapped around her bent legs and her head resting on her knees.

His heart skipped a beat. Was she hurt?

Fortune nickered when Jasper tugged on the reins and he slid out of the saddle before the horse had stopped completely.

Lynna looked up at him. Her lashes were spiked with tears and her eyes were puffy and red. She'd been crying. It tore at his insides to see her like that, but she didn't seem hurt. Relief overwhelmed him.

He dropped to his knees at her side and before he even had a chance to think about what he was doing, he reached around her and drew her toward him.

Lynna sagged into Jasper's arms, reveling in his warmth and his touch. She thought she'd finished crying and feeling sorry for herself, but tears again spilled over and trickled down her cheeks.

"Are you all right?"

Her head snuggled into the side of his neck. His breath tickled her cheek. His unique scent washed over her, giving her a sense of comfort she'd never had before.

She nodded, pulling back until he released her. "I'm fine, other than my feet." She raised her foot off the ground a few inches. "I think I have blisters on top of blisters."

"We'll take care of that when we get you home," he said, "but is that … I mean … are you okay otherwise?"

"I'm fine," she said. She tried to smile, but the best she could offer him was a faint twitch of her lips.

"Then why are you crying?" he asked.

She sniffled. "I am not. I just got some dust in my eyes."

He gazed at her for a few moments, and she knew that he knew she was lying. Right now, she didn't care.

"Mrs. Platt told me you'd gone looking for work. You could have waited. I would have taken you."

"I didn't want to wait. I want to get on with my life, and I can't do that without work."

He nodded. Did he really understand, or was he merely trying to soothe her ruffled feathers?

"Want to tell me what happened in town?"

She shook her head in resignation and let out a sigh. "I went to every shop, every business. No one would hire me."

"I'm sorry," he said.

She looked up at him. The tone of his voice told her he was sincere.

"There was only one place left that I hadn't tried."

"The Pleasure Palace."

She nodded. "I did. Two women who … work there … were on the balcony." She didn't go into detail about what the women had told her.

"And?"

"They told me who to see and I went to the door." She shook her head, annoyed and frustrated with herself for her high moral standards. "I couldn't go inside."

She sensed his relief in the way his body seemed to relax against hers. "Thank God," he whispered.

"I was prepared to do whatever it took, but when the time came, I just couldn't."

Reaching out, he cradled her jaw in his hands and brought her face up so that she could meet his eyes. "You don't know how glad I am to hear you say that."

For a long moment, neither of them spoke. The air seemed to spark between them and his head lowered toward hers.

She couldn't move. Didn't want to move. And suddenly, his lips touched hers.

CHAPTER 7

asper was kissing her! Hubert, her situation, the world and everything in it – they all fell away and all she could think, all she could feel, was the heat flowing through her as his lips slanted across hers and his arms enfolded her once again.

She'd never been kissed like this – the way she'd heard a man kissed a woman he cared for, and it was more, much more than she'd ever imagined.

Her arms slid around his waist and her fingers dug into the thin fabric of his shirt. She heard him suck in a breath and the kiss deepened, both demanding and gentle at the same time. Her body pressed against his, his heartbeat … or was it hers … pounding in her ears.

Nothing she'd ever experienced in her life had affected her like this. Frightening, but exhilarating and exciting and oh, so wonderful.

Kissing was the beginning of what happened between men and women in the marriage bed. A thought flitted through her mind that if the sensations she felt deep inside were so strong with just a kiss, she couldn't imagine what more could feel like.

But Heaven help her, she wanted to find out.

Jasper released her, his breathing ragged.

He gazed down at her, her lips swollen, her expression filled with wonder. Had she never been kissed before? He hoped not. He hoped he'd been the first man to taste her lips, to feel her melt into him and respond the way she had. Her breaths escaped in short, small gasps, and as he looked at her, her fingers reached for her lips and traced the path his mouth had taken only seconds before.

"I'd say I'm sorry," he said, his voice gravelly, "but I'm not. I've wanted to do that for a long time. I should have asked permission first, though, and for that I do apologize."

A soft smile creased her lips. "I would have granted it," she said softly, her cheeks pinking at the admission.

The kiss had been everything and more. It was everything he wanted. She was everything he wanted, now and for the rest of his life.

All he had to do was convince her to stay in Rocky Ridge.

Jasper gazed out his office window, but barely even noticed the leaves beginning to fall on the aspens in the yard. He hadn't been able to get Lynna out of his mind since their kiss. Even the ranch hands had noticed how distracted he'd been that morning while they hauled hay into one of the barns.

He hadn't seen Lynna since he'd brought her back to the ranch the day before. She'd been unusually quiet on the ride back to the ranch, and as soon as he'd helped her out of the wagon, she'd hurried inside, pleading a raging headache. She'd gone to her room and had even refused supper.

Mrs. Platt had taken a tray upstairs, but when he'd questioned her about Lynna's sudden illness, she'd muttered something about her needing some peace and quiet.

She hadn't appeared at breakfast, either. Mrs. Platt had told him she wasn't feeling well, but it wasn't serious. Jasper suspected it had nothing to do with illness, and everything to do with their kiss the day before.

The memory of that kiss and what it had meant to him had kept him awake most of the night. His hand reached into his pocket and pulled out the envelope containing the letter he'd written to Edith. He took the single page out and read it again.

If he hadn't taken Deirdre's package to the train depot... But he had, and it had changed everything.

He'd had the letter in his pocket to mail, but something had stopped him. At some point during the long night, he'd figured out what that something was, and he sure couldn't send it now. He couldn't marry Edith, not when Lynna had captured his heart. Even if Lynna never loved him back, it wouldn't be fair to Edith to marry her, knowing he'd never be able to return her love.

Suddenly, he heard a soft knock on his office door. He spun around at the sound. "Come in."

The door opened and Lynna walked in. Even though she seemed a bit pale, she was still the most beautiful woman he'd ever seen. She was wearing a pale green striped cotton dress that hugged her curves and revealed her creamy skin of her neck. Desire surged through him and he wanted nothing more than to wrap her in his arms and kiss her senseless, but if her "illness" had been caused by their kiss, which he suspected it had, he didn't dare risk it.

He tossed the letter onto his desk and moved toward her. "Good morning," he said. "Mrs. Platt said you weren't well. How are you feeling now?"

"I'm fine, thank you. I would like to talk to you if you have time. If you're busy, perhaps we could speak later."

"Sit down." Jasper gestured to a padded armchair near his desk. "I've wanted to speak to you, too."

Lynna's brows arched and her eyes widened. "Oh? You have?"

"Yes, but you go first."

Lynna perched on the edge of the chair and folded her hands in her lap. "I realize my presence here is an inconvenience," she began, "and again, I want to thank you for your generosity and hospitality since I found myself in such a predicament."

Jasper waved away her gratitude and smiled down at her. "You are definitely not an inconvenience—"

"You're very kind, but I can't impose on you any longer than necessary. I've given it a lot of thought, and I've come to a decision. But I would like to ask one last favor."

"What's that?"

"I need to acquire skills that will help me to find employment when I leave Rocky Ridge. I've already spoken to Mrs. Platt, and she has agreed to teach me how to cook, do laundry, clean, everything a house-keeper does, if you don't mind."

Jasper's stomach flipped. He'd hoped that maybe, just maybe, she'd been taken aback by their kiss the day before because it had affected her. And that she'd realized she loved him as much as he loved her.

Her words destroyed that hope. "You're still planning to leave."

She nodded. "Why wouldn't I? Hubert or his men will come after me. I know you don't think so, but I know him and I know he'll never rest until I'm punished. So the farther I get away from Hubert and his men, the safer I'll be."

"You're safe here," Jasper insisted.

Lynna shook her head. "No, I'm not, and ..." She

looked away, but not before Jasper saw her eyes grow bright with unshed tears. Then she raised her head and met his gaze squarely. "The other day when you went to the livery, you risked your life because of me. I won't allow anyone else to ever put themselves in danger for me, so the sooner I leave here, the better. So, do you have any objection to Mrs. Platt teaching me?"

His insides twisted at the thought of her leaving, but he shook his head. "No, if that's what you want," he said, "but out of curiosity, what were your plans if I didn't go along with this plan?"

"Then I'd leave today."

"Where would you go?"

"It doesn't matter. I wouldn't tell you. That way, when Hubert's men track me here, you won't have to lie to protect me."

Jasper raked his hand through his hair. "That's the most asinine reasoning I've ever heard."

She nodded, her lips narrowing. "Asinine or not, it's what I would do. I admit, however, that I'm glad I don't have to resort to that. Now I'll let you get back to your work and I'll tell Mrs. Platt you approve."

His heartbeat hammered behind his ribs. He'd given permission, but he didn't exactly approve. He had another idea, one that he much preferred. She could stay in Rocky Ridge – with him – and even if Hubert came after her, he couldn't force her to go back and marry him.

He reached out and took her hand in his. He

waited for her reaction. If she pulled away, he'd know her answer before he even asked the question. She didn't, and that gave him hope they could have a future together. "There is another option," he said.

"There is?" Optimism shone in her eyes.

His throat dried up, and he wondered for a few seconds if he could even get the words out. Finally, he sucked in a calming breath. His voice was low and gruff when he finally spoke. "You could marry me."

Marry him? Was he serious? Why would he offer to marry a woman he barely knew? It made no sense.

Besides, had he forgotten she'd run away to escape marriage? Well, to be honest, she'd only run away to escape marriage to Hubert, not marriage itself. But still, she was finally going to be independent, to live her own life. She wasn't about to marry a man she barely knew, no matter how handsome he was or how kind he seemed to be.

Why, he could be as bad or worse than Hubert for all she knew. Even as the thought flitted through her mind, she didn't believe it. She didn't know him well, but so far, he hadn't given her any reason to think he was anything but a gentleman. After all, he'd rescued her, fed her, given her a place to stay and gone out of his way to try to help her find work.

If she was going to marry, her instinct told her she could do much worse than marry Jasper.

"Did I hear you correctly?" she asked. "You're proposing marriage?"

"I am."

"Why?"

"It's time for me to get married. Seems like you could use a husband. If you're married, there's no way you could be forced to go back and marry your fiancé."

While what he was saying was true, it wasn't a solution she was willing to consider. "So you'd marry me to protect me from Hubert?"

"Well … yes. It would give us both what we want."

"I appreciate the offer, but no. I'm going to be moving on as soon as Mrs. Platt teaches me enough that I can find employment somewhere."

"It's a good solution," he insisted.

"It is a solution. Whether it's good or not is debatable. But the answer is still no. I'm not planning to get married in the near future. If and when I do marry, I'll marry a man I have feelings for. Not for convenience or security, but for love. Nothing less."

His chest felt as if a giant bubble had burst inside him. Disappointment filled him. He'd thought … he'd hoped … she cared about him, but it looked like she'd rather deal with her fiancé than be with him. "Well," he choked out, doing his best not to show how much she'd hurt him, "if you change your mind …"

She got to her feet. "I won't. Now if you'll excuse me, I believe Mrs. Platt has some bread dough waiting for me. She wants to teach me how to knead it, whatever that means."

~

Lynna punched at the ball of dough on the counter, gaining a hmpph! from Mrs. Platt. "You aren't in a boxing match, Lynna," she pointed out.

"Sorry," Lynna said quietly, her gaze landing on the deep well in the center of the dough. "My mind was wandering."

"Well, I feel sorry for whoever you're pretending is on the other end of that fist."

Lynna let out a tiny chuckle and brushed the flour off her hand.

"Just put it back in the bowl and cover it until it rises again."

While she followed Mrs. Platt's instructions, her thoughts returned to the conversation she'd had with Jasper a few minutes before.

Was she wrong to reject his proposal? Was it foolish of her to believe true love was waiting for her somewhere out there?

Not that she even knew what true love felt like. Would she even recognize it? She doubted very much that her parents had ever been in love, and every other married couple she was acquainted with didn't show any affection for each other.

Was there even really such a thing as true love? Was she searching for something that didn't exist.

Jasper seemed like a good man. She already liked him. In fact, she liked him more than any other man she'd ever known.

That was something, at least. He was kind, obviously treated people well or Mrs. Platt wouldn't have stayed so long. Perhaps she was making a mistake in refusing him so quickly. She could have told him she'd consider it, and had time to really get to know him. It would also have given her time to find employment if things didn't work out.

But most of all — by refusing him, was she giving up a home and security for something that she might never find, even if real love did exist?

CHAPTER 8

*K*eeping a house running smoothly is a lot harder than it looks, Lynna muttered to Jasper's empty office as yet again, she whisked the broom across the wooden plank floor, gathering up clumps of dirt and sending small clouds of dust into the air. This was the third time that day she'd swept both his office and the pathway between it and the front door. It seemed that Jasper and his men didn't even stop to think about wiping their feet on the mat on the porch before they dragged the dirt in from outside.

In the days since she'd started helping Mrs. Platt, she'd gained new respect for those men and women who toiled long hours to keep a house clean and their employers fed and clothed in clean clothes.

She swept the dirt into the dustpan and spilled it into the wastebasket beside his desk. As she straightened, her elbow caught a pile of correspondence piled on top of a book on the desk. The book fell, the papers scattering and fluttering to the floor.

Lynna muttered to herself as she leaned the broom and dustpan against the wall. Then she crouched and began picking up the papers. A few were wrinkled, as if the letters had been read several times, and two bills from an equipment supplier back east had round stains, as if Jasper had rested his coffee mugs on them.

Once she'd put the papers back where they'd been before she knocked them off, she took one last look under the chairs and the other furniture in the room to check for anything she'd missed.

A corner of a piece of paper under his desk caught her attention. She bent down and plucked it out and was about to put it with the others in the pile when the heavy pen strokes stopped her. "My dearest Edith," it began.

Lynna knew she shouldn't read any further. She was invading Jasper's privacy, but she couldn't help herself.

A chill washed over her as her eyes skimmed over the words on the page. The woman and Jasper had a relationship, a close personal relationship.

The letter was a marriage proposal – to another woman.

Lynna struggled to draw in a deep breath and an ache filled her chest. Her vision blurred as tears filled her eyes and trickled down her cheeks. She'd been wrong about him. He was no different than every other man – than Hubert. He'd hidden it better than the other men she'd known back east, but deep down, he was the same. What had he planned to do, marry both of them? Keep one wife back east and one here on his ranch in Colorado? Or was he proposing to both and marrying the first woman to accept? Either way, he was definitely not the man she thought he was. He was a cad, a rogue, a miscreant. Every vile name she could think of flashed into her brain.

She couldn't tell him she'd read his letter, but now, knowing the kind of man he really was, she wanted nothing to do with him. She couldn't leave yet, though. She still had so much to learn from Mrs. Platt. So, she decided, the best way to handle it would be to avoid him as much as possible until she was confident she was capable enough to go out on her own. Then she'd leave and never have to see him again.

Her heart constricted at the thought, and that angered her even more than she'd let herself love him in the first place.

A gasp escaped her. She loved him! Until this moment, she'd fought against it, denied it to herself. But the truth was … somehow she'd fallen in love with this man who had just broken her heart.

"Are you almost finished in here? I have some things to take care of."

Startled, she shoved the letter into the pocket of her skirt and spun around. She was tempted to throw the letter in his face, to demand an explanation. She resisted. Impulsiveness wasn't in her nature. She'd only once acted without thinking it through and considering the consequences, and look how that had turned out.

She glared at him, anger … and hurt … filling every cell in her body. "I'm sure you do," she snapped as she brushed past him and hurried away.

Jasper set his fork down on the table and looked up at Lynna bustling around the kitchen. "That was a fine meal, Lynna. You should have eaten, too. I hope you're not getting sick."

"I'm fine. Not hungry is all." She turned her back on him, but not before he noticed the faint blush on her cheeks.

He shook his head. What was wrong with her? She'd made excuse after excuse to avoid eating her meals with him for four days. She'd suddenly found chores to do in the evenings so their backgammon games were a thing of the past, and it seemed she made a point of not even being in the same room with him as much as she could manage it.

She was furious with him. That much was plain to see. What wasn't plain to see was why. He couldn't remember doing or saying anything that would make her act the way she was. And the way she looked at him … as if he was lower than a rattlesnake.

He'd done everything he could to draw her out, to

get her to tell him what was bothering her, but she'd said there was nothing wrong, then found an excuse to get away from him.

Tonight was the first time she'd made a complete meal by herself and Mrs. Platt had made him promise he'd be complimentary even if the food tasted like pig slop.

Thankfully, he didn't have to lie. The beef was a little tough, but the potatoes and cabbage were tasty, and even Lynna couldn't destroy berries and cream.

"I'll take care of the dishes since you cooked," Mrs. Platt announced as she rose from the table and began clearing. Turning to Lynna, she asked, "Did you use the last of the flour for the gravy?"

Lynna nodded.

"I'm going into town tomorrow," Jasper put in. "Lynna, why don't you come with me and you can go to the mercantile to stock up."

"No … I—"

"Good idea," Mrs. Platt interrupted. "I'll make a list."

"Mrs. Platt," Lynna began, "you know better than I do what supplies we need. I'm happy to stay here and do the chores so you can go."

The housekeeper scraped the leftover food off her plate into the bucket beside the dry sink. "Nonsense. You need to get out of the house and get some fresh air."

Jasper leaned back in his chair and folded his arms across his chest. His mood brightened. Hopefully, when she couldn't run away or find an excuse not to talk to him, he could get to the bottom of why she was so mad at him.

"I really wish you'd tell me what I did," Jasper said the next afternoon when they were on their way back from town.

Lynna sent him a scathing look. Oh, she'd tell him all right. One day, when she had sorted her feelings out herself, she'd tell him that he was a lying, lowdown polecat he was, but not before she was ready.

"Looks like we have company," he commented as the wagon crested the last small hill and looked down on the ranch in the valley below.

She didn't answer. She had no interest in who was visiting him. Instead, she focused on the lush green grass and the cattle in the distance.

A few minutes later, he drew the wagon to a halt in front of the stairs leading to the front porch of the ranch house.

Lynna knew he'd come around the wagon to help her down and she couldn't stand the thought of him touching her. The last time he had … Her throat tightened at the memory of their kiss, how tender he'd been, how she'd loved being in his arms.

She tripped on her dress and almost fell head first into the dirt in her haste to get out of the wagon before he had a chance to help her. She did manage to right herself before he reached her and raced up the stairs and threw the door open.

She hurried inside and was half way up the stairs to her bedroom when she heard Mrs. Platt's voice calling her from the parlor. "Lynna, someone's here to see you."

CHAPTER 9

"Hello, Lynna."

The room swam in front of Lynna's eyes when she entered the room a few seconds later and saw the man standing by the fireplace, his hands clasped together behind his back. His brown frock coat strained against his protruding belly, and his fleshy neck spilled over the collar of his snow-white shirt. She hadn't thought it possible for the man to gain ever more weight, but she'd been wrong.

She'd known this day would come, but she'd never expected Hubert to be so brazen as to show up at Jasper's ranch as if he was an invited guest.

Mrs. Platt stood beside him, a wide smile on her face.

Lynna had never told Mrs. Platt the circumstances of her sudden appearance at the ranch, but she'd assumed Jasper had explained. Apparently he hadn't.

If he had, she was sure Mrs. Platt wouldn't have welcomed him into the house.

"Mr. Deline has come all the way from Boston to see you." The housekeeper's voice broke into Lynna's thoughts. "Isn't that wonderful?"

A smile creased Hubert's lips, but the icy glare Lynna saw in his eyes sent a tremor of fear through her.

"It's good to see you, Lynna," he said. His voice dripped with honey, but Lynna knew him well enough to recognize the sarcastic undertones.

She couldn't answer past the dryness in her throat.

Mrs. Platt turned her attention to Hubert. "I'll just go and get the tea now that Lynna's here and you two can catch up."

"Thank you, Mrs. Platt," Huber replied, his eyes never leaving Lynna's face. "That's very kind of you."

Moments later, they were alone.

"I must say, you do look different," he said, his gaze raking over her and settling on her breasts. "You've gained a little weight, and it's very becoming."

Lynna knew exactly what he was referring to. Deirdre's dresses were quite snug, and she quickly folded her arms across her chest. "What ... what are you doing here?"

Hubert crossed the room toward her. "I've come to take you back where you belong."

Lynna took a step backward to avoid his touch. "I'm not going anywhere."

"You've had your fun," he snapped. "You humiliated your parents and embarrassed me in front of my friends. I've had enough of your nonsense. Now you'll come back with me and be suitably repentant."

Her heart hammered in her chest, but she clenched her hands together and faced him squarely. "I'm not going to marry you, Hubert. That's why I left, and I haven't changed my mind. In fact, I'm happier here than I have been for quite some time." That wasn't true … at least not now …, but she couldn't let Hubert know that.

Again, Hubert closed in on her. She retreated another few steps. He advanced, until finally, her back collided with the wall. He leaned close to her. His breath slithered along her skin as he whispered in her ear. "Once we're married, you'll learn it's not wise to reject me." His hand cupped her chin and then slid down until his large beefy fingers stretched around her neck.

She wasn't sure if she imagined the faint pressure of his fingers on her throat, but the threat was very real.

Suddenly, a door slammed and heavy footsteps crossed the wooden floor.

Jasper's gaze took in the sight before him. Lynna was against the wall near the fireplace, both fear and something else shining in her eyes. A man towered over her, his hand resting on her neck.

Fury, the likes of which he'd never known before, surged through him.

"Get away from her!"

His blood rushed into his face and his heart raced. His fists clenched at his sides, and it took every ounce of self-control he could muster not to draw his six-shooter and kill the man right on the spot.

"Are you all right, Lynna?" he asked, forcing a calmness into his voice that belied the emotions raging inside.

She nodded, but didn't speak.

Hubert backed away from her, holding his hands up in mock surrender. "I apologize. It's not what it looked like, I assure you. We were just getting reacquainted, weren't we, Lynna?"

She didn't answer, focusing more on staying upright since her knees were shaking so badly she had to move to grasp the back of a chair.

Jasper took a step toward Hubert. The two men were about the same height, but Hubert outweighed him by at least forty or fifty pounds. Still, Jasper was pretty sure the man didn't have an ounce of muscle beneath the flab that strained against his coat. "I'd advise you to leave now before I have you arrested," Jasper warned.

Hubert had the nerve to look shocked. "Arrested? For what? I haven't committed any crime. I merely came to visit an old friend. Surely that's not against the law, even here in this Godforsaken place."

"No, it isn't, but trespassing on my land is. You're not welcome here, and I have the right to shoot you right here and now if I want to. So I'm telling you again, leave now and don't come back."

The two men glared at each other, neither of them ready to back down.

"Please, Hubert," Lynna burst in, "just go. I'm not going back. Not now. Not ever. I'm sorry if I embarrassed you in front of your friends—"

"Embarrassed? You made me the laughing stock of the entire town."

"Again, I apologize, but I had no choice."

"You should have done what your parents agreed to."

"That's the point. They agreed to the marriage. I didn't."

"I practically supported your entire family for months leading up to the wedding."

"I didn't know anything about that until the day of the wedding. You tried to buy me, and my parents allowed it."

"How much?" Jasper interrupted. "How much do you want to pay off what you gave her family?"

Hubert turned toward Jasper and laughed. "You think I want money? I have more money than you'll ever have and more than I will ever be able to spend. I don't need money. I want the wife I paid for."

"That's not going to happen. Now for the last

time, leave," Jasper warned. His fingers flexed and his hand automatically drifted toward the gun in his holster. "Now. Or you'll be leaving in a pine box."

Hubert looked at Lynna, a wicked grin on his face as he picked up his hat and rested it on his head. At that moment, Mrs. Platt came in with a tray holding a silver tea service, cups and saucers and a plate of sugar cookies. "You're not staying for tea, Mr. Deline?

"My apologies, but I'm afraid I have to leave." Turning to Lynna, he added, "I'll give your regards to your parents if I see them again. I do worry, though, how they're going to survive now that your father will be losing his job and won't be able to find another?"

"Are you sure you're all right?" Jasper asked as the front door clicked shut behind Hubert. "Did he hurt you?"

Lynna shook her head. No, he hadn't physically injured her, but what he'd done was worse. Much worse. He hadn't had to verbally threaten her parents, but she'd gotten the message. Had her family sunk to such depths they couldn't even support themselves without his help? If that was the case, could she really desert them? She hadn't given it any thought when she'd decided to escape the wedding, but now ...

Tears filled her eyes and spilled down her cheeks. Jasper crossed the room toward her, and even though he'd broken her heart, she couldn't resist when he reached for her. She sank into his warmth, her tears soaking the front of his shirt.

"What's going on?" Mrs. Platt asked, still holding the tea tray.

Lynna heard Jasper's voice, felt the vibration as he explained the situation to Mrs. Platt. "Oh, I canna believe I let that man into the house – and even offered him tea."

Lynna sniffled and raised her head. "It's not your fault, Mrs. Platt," she said softly. "You didn't know."

"Because nobody in this house tells me anything."

"I should have," Lynna admitted, "but I didn't want you to think badly of me."

"Och, that's silly. I wouldn't have thought you were anything but a smart young woman. Why would a pretty girl like you want to be saddled with an old man like him?"

"But now he can destroy my family, and I have no doubt he will."

Jasper jammed the pitchfork into the pile of hay and tossed it into the stall. Every nerve ending was alert, his muscles tense. He'd been looking over his shoulder for almost a week now, and he even though he hadn't seen hide nor hair of Hubert Deline since he'd threatened the man, Jasper wasn't convinced he wasn't lurking somewhere nearby.

Every morning, he'd ridden into town and

stopped in at the sheriff's office to speak to Zane Morgan. And every time, Zane had assured him there'd been no sign of Deline still being in town and that he'd ride out to the ranch if he saw or heard anything about him.

So why couldn't Jasper relax?

Because deep down he knew this wasn't over. His gut had served him well over the years, and he'd learned – sometimes the hard way – to trust it. And right now, his gut was screaming at him to pay attention.

Still, he couldn't spend every minute of every day with Lynna, much as he'd like to. And it wasn't only to keep her safe. At first, he'd thought it was nothing more than lust. He'd been without a woman for a long time, and her angelic face and the tight-fitting clothes she was wearing made his blood heat. Sure, he wanted her in his bed, but it was more than that.

He'd never felt this way before. When he was with her, it felt as if his insides were smiling.

She'd been standoffish with him for a few days before Deline showed up, but by the way she'd clung to him after Deline left, he'd thought she'd forgiven him for whatever he'd done to make her angry. She hadn't resisted, and she'd actually wrapped her arms around his waist. Even when she stopped crying, she'd stayed in his arms until Mrs. Platt had come back with the tea.

Since that day, she'd been quieter than usual. She was worried about her family's well-being. He knew that. But was she worried enough that she was considering going back with Deline? From what she'd told him, the man had more money than the federal bank. He could provide for her and her family.

Not only would that be a dangerous mistake, but it would mean he'd never see her again. Every time the thought registered in his brain, his chest tightened and his stomach twisted.

The man was violent. He'd known that the minute he'd come into the room and seen his hand on her neck. No, he hadn't been hurting her, but all it would have taken was a slight tension in his fingers and he could have choked the life out of her. And if he hadn't shown up when he did …

Short of keeping her locked up somewhere, Jasper couldn't stop her if she decided to go with Deline. All he could do was hope she wouldn't. Even if she left Rocky Ridge the way she planned to, he'd rather she did that, even if it meant he'd lost her forever.

Mrs. Platt hurried out of the mercantile, stopping just long enough to put her packages in the wagon before turning to Lynna. "I'm just going to check if my new hat is ready. Jasper said he'd meet us at the café when we're done. You don't mind waiting a few minutes, do you?"

Lynna shook her head. "I'll wait for you right here," she said as she climbed into the wagon.

"Fine."

Lynna grinned as she watched Mrs. Platt practically run down the boardwalk toward the milliner's shop. Soon her attention was caught up in a squabble between two children that had them rolling around in the dirt for some time before they got up and walked away together.

She chuckled. It was a shame adults didn't forgive so easily.

She glanced down the street toward the café. Was Jasper already there waiting for them? Her heart swelled with love, a love that was so painful. He was going to marry another woman. Had the written the letter before or after he'd proposed to her?

It didn't matter, she chided herself. She had to leave. It was time.

She'd learned how to do laundry, and change linens, and all the other chores that kept a house spotless. She might never be the cook Mrs. Platt was, but she'd practiced her until she could make several dishes. She'd even stayed up late at night copying the housekeeper's recipes to take with her.

She could survive. Her heart was broken, but she would survive.

"Miss?" A young voice called out. She turned to see a boy about seven years old racing toward her.

"Yes?"

"Mr. … Morton …" The boy scratched his head, sending his dark curls bouncing. "Nah, that wasn't it … Mr. …"

"Morrison?" Lynna questioned.

The boys eyes widened. "Yep. That's it. Anyway, he said he had something to show you at the hotel and to come right away."

"The hotel?"

The boy's head bobbed. "He even gave me a penny."

"Thank you," Lynna replied absently. She looked toward the new four-story building that Jasper had told her had been built only five years before. What on earth could Jasper have to show her?

She glanced around. People wandered about, wagons rolled by. The street was busy. Jasper had made her promise not to go off by herself, but surely with so many people around, she wouldn't be in any danger.

"Can I go now?" The boy interrupted her pondering.

"Yes … no …" Lynna looked down at the boy. There was one way to make sure it was Jasper who'd sent the message.

"What's your name?"

"Georgie," the boy replied.

She climbed out of the wagon and crouched to be at eye level with the boy. "What did the man look like, Georgie?"

The little boy's mouth twisted and his forehead crinkled. "I don't 'member. He was big though, and his hair was brown. He had a gun, too."

"I see." It sounded like Jasper, and she knew Hubert never carried a gun. "Thank you."

The boy raced off and Lynna climbed out of the wagon and made her way toward the milliner's shop to tell Mrs. Platt where she was going.

A few minutes later, she was crossing the street toward the hotel.

She paused for a few moments to let her eyes grow accustomed to the dim light inside the hotel when she entered. A young couple was sitting at a table in the corner of the dining room to the right, but the lobby was empty. Strange, she thought. Surely someone should be manning the desk in case guests came in. And where was Jasper?

She stepped around the desk and peeked through an open doorway, thinking he might be inside with the hotel's proprietor. Suddenly, an arm snaked around her body, lifting her off her feet and pressing her body back against a hard wall of muscle.

She opened her mouth to scream, but before she could force a sound past her dry throat, a hand covered her mouth.

CHAPTER 10

"Stop fighting, Lynna. I don't want you to get hurt. It would be a shame to if that pretty face of yours got marked."

The voice – Hubert's voice - came from somewhere in the distance, which meant it was likely Bart holding her.

Panic surged through her. Her knees wobbled, but Bart's iron grip kept her upright. Still, she struggled, kicking and squirming against his hold on her.

What was Hubert planning to do with her? He couldn't keep her prisoner for the rest of her life, and he must realize she'd escape again as soon as she had an opportunity. Unless … her throat squeezed shut with fear. Unless he was going to kill her.

Lynna's heel connected with Bart's shin. "Arrgh!" he cried out. He let loose with a string of swear words but didn't loosen his hold.

"I won't tell you again," Hubert said calmly,

moving so that he was in her line of vision. "Stop struggling, or Bart will be forced to take more drastic measures to shut you up."

All rational thought had left her mind during her struggle, but one thought did take hold. Hubert was arrogant. If she played into his arrogance, he might lower his guard.

She nodded, and with a slight wave from Hubert, Bart took his hand away. Lynna sucked in a few breaths to calm herself.

"In case you think Morrison will swoop in like a hero and rescue you, it's not going to happen. The boy is on his way to tell him that you're going to see about a position at the hotel and you'll walk back to the ranch when you're finished. By the time he realizes you're not coming back, we'll be miles away from here." He grinned then. "And you'll be wishing you'd never left Boston."

"I'll … I'll go with you," she said, pouring as much resignation and defeat into her voice as she could. "Just don't hurt me, please."

"That's better. Now, let's walk out and get into the wagon without any trouble."

Bart pulled a gun out of his holster and moved behind her. She didn't have to see it to know it was pointed at her back.

Hubert was going to kill her. Another 'accident'? Or would she suddenly become ill with some incurable disease?

A sense of calm washed over her. If she was going

to die, it might as well be sooner rather than later. Once she got in the wagon with him and they left town, her life was over, even if she did survive to reach Boston.

She didn't know what to do, only that she had to try something before she got into that wagon. She had no weapon, nothing to use. Her blood pounded in her ears and her knees trembled so badly as she walked out of the hotel in front of Bart and Hubert that she thought she might faint.

An idea burst into her brain. It likely wouldn't work, but it was worth a try.

She wobbled, letting one leg buckle. "Ohh …"

"What's the matter?" Hubert came to stand beside her.

"I feel … faint …"

As she expected, Hubert grabbed her elbow and pushed her forward through the door. Again, she let her knees unlock and relaxed her body, just enough that he tried to steady her. He looked behind him for a second or two to make sure Bart was following with the gun pointed at her. That was all the time she needed.

Tugging her arm out of his grip, she twisted around in front of him so that he was between her and Bart's gun and ran screaming into the street.

Gunshots rang in her ears, and she heard somebody shout. "Get out of the way!"

She looked in the direction of the voice. A wagon carrying a load of lumber was barreling toward her, the driver tugging furiously on the reins of the horses pulling it.

She froze.

Jasper took out his pocket watch for the fourth time. Where were Lynna and Mrs. Platt? He was sure he'd told them to meet him in the café at one o'clock and he'd been waiting almost a half hour.

"Sure you wouldn't like a refill of your coffee while you wait?"

Jasper turned toward the waitress standing beside the table, a metal coffee pot in her hand.

"No, thanks," he replied. "I'm sure they'll be here any minute."

The waitress wandered off, leaving Jasper to nurse the remains of his coffee while he watched for them through the window.

As he looked on, he saw people beginning to run toward a commotion at the other end of town.

Getting up, he went to the café's door and asked a man hurrying toward the scene. "What's going on?"

"Don't rightly know," the man said, "but there was bullets flyin' and somebody got run down by a wagon. Gonna go find out for myself." The man hurried off.

Unease prickled Jasper's skin. He had no reason to believe the situation had anything to do with Lynna, but he couldn't shake the feeling that he needed to find her. Now.

He tossed a dollar bill on the table and grabbed his hat, then raced out the door and headed toward the crowd in the middle of the street.

"What's happening?" he asked a scruffy cowboy when he reached the back of the crowd.

"Lady got hit by a wagon," the cowboy said. "Don't look good."

Jasper's heartbeat pounded in his ears and his stomach seized in a knot as he elbowed his way through the crowd. He had to see for himself.

"Let the doc through!" a voice shouted.

The crowd parted. Grace Leonard, one of the two doctors in town, hurried past him. As the people closed in again, Jasper caught a glimpse of blue.

Lynna was wearing a blue dress.

He pushed his way past two men to the front. His heart stopped. Lynna lay in a crumpled heap on the ground, blood soaking into the dirt beneath her. She wasn't moving.

A hammer pounded in Lynna's head, and every breath sent pain rocketing through her body. But she must be alive. Surely if she was dead she wouldn't hurt so much.

For that few seconds before the wagon hit her, she'd been frozen in place, unable to move. She remembered the driving calling out, and she'd seen him try to rein in his team, but with the weight of the lumber behind him, he couldn't stop in time or veer away.

She'd been sure she was going to die.

"Lynna, honey, can you hear me?"

Jasper's voice. Beside her. His hand was wrapped around hers, his warmth flowing through her.

She tried to open her mouth to speak. It took too much effort, but after two tries, she did manage to open her eyes for a second or two until they stung so badly she closed them again.

"Grace!" Jasper shouted

The sound was an explosion in her head. She groaned.

"Sorry," he whispered. "I'm just so glad you're waking up."

She opened her eyes again. They didn't sting as much this time. Carefully, she moved her head to see Jasper sitting in a hardback chair beside the bed. She had no idea where she was, but she didn't care. "How long …?"

"Just a few hours, but they were the longest hours of my life. I thought I'd lost you."

"You … didn't."

She tried to move, let out a tortured moan, and gave up. Even letting herself sink back onto the mattress was agonizing.

"You broke a few ribs, you've got a cut on your head and a lot of bruises."

"Hubert … he—"

"He won't be bothering you again. Zane arrested him. Charged him with murder, attempted murder—"

"Murder? He killed somebody because of me?" She couldn't bear it if she was the cause of someone dying.

He shook his head. "No. Bart Abrahams turned on him. Told Zane he'd seen Deline murder his wife. If it's true, Deline will hang and Abrahams will go to prison for his part in what happened to you."

"It's really over?"

He smiled gently and squeezed her hand. "It's over. You don't have to be afraid anymore."

Silence hung over the room while the news sank into her mind. "So I can go home."

She didn't want to, but what else could she do? Stay in Rocky Ridge and watch Jasper build a life with another woman?

Her throat tightened with sadness and a different kind of pain enveloped her. Not pain from her injuries. Broken bones would mend. Bruises would disappear. This pain, the pain of losing the only man she'd ever love, would never heal no matter how long she lived.

"Do you want to go back to Boston?" Jasper asked.

Should she tell him how she felt about him, even though he was going to marry someone else?

"No. I really don't."

She thought she saw him smile, but it disappeared so quickly she thought she might have imagined it.

"Then you have time to think about what you want to do while you get better," he said.

She didn't time. She knew exactly what would make her happy – staying in Rocky Ridge. With Jasper.

But that wasn't to be.

"I don't have to think about it," she said quietly, watching his face, memorizing every detail for the long, lonely life waiting for her. "I'll be leaving as soon as I'm able," she said, her voice breaking. She couldn't bear to stay and watch him build a life with another woman.

"I see." He got up and crossed to the window. His shoulders slumped and his head bowed for what seemed like an eternity before he turned back to face her.

"Would it make a difference if I asked you not to go?"

"Why? What possible reason could I have to stay?"

"Because ..." He came back to the bed, dropped into the chair and took both her hands in his. His work-roughened thumbs grazed her palms, sending a shiver through her. "Because I love you and I can't imagine my life without you here."

How she'd longed to hear those words before ... before she'd found the letter with his proposal to another woman.

Now, they were a reminder that he wasn't the man she'd thought he was. How could she love a man like him? That she did filled her with fury – at herself. How pathetic she was.

But she still had her pride. "I won't be your mistress."

"Mistress? Why would you be my mistress? I proposed to you once, and that proposal is still open if you're willing."

She let out a bitter laugh. "You honestly think I'd marry you now that I know what kind of man you really are?"

"What kind of man do you think I am?"

"A womanizer at the very least, a bigamist at most."

"I think I need to get Grace to check your head again. You're not making any sense."

Even though she was in pain, even though her heart was breaking, she was quite sane and rational. Anger built inside, anger she'd held on to for far too long. "Don't deny it," she spat out. "I found your letter to the woman you *also* intend to marry."

"What … oh …" He flushed. "You did?"

"I did. I was cleaning your office and my elbow knocked some papers off your desk. I saw it when I was picking them up. I couldn't believe you'd proposed to me and yet you were writing to another woman to ask her to marry you, too."

He chuckled then, only fueling her anger.

Her head pounded, and she could practically feel her blood boiling. How dare he laugh at her? What a cad he was! "Why are you laughing?"

"So that's why you've been giving me the cold shoulder for the past few days," he said, his laughter dying out.

"What did you expect me to do? Offer my congratulations?"

He shook his head. "I'm sorry you found that letter."

Every breath was agonizing, but she couldn't help herself. "Why? So you could marry us both? What were you planning to do, keep us in separate towns?

Travel between us with some cockamamie story about why you were away so much?"

"Stop!"

The command in his tone did steal her speech. She slumped back on the pillow and looked away. "Just go away and leave me alone."

She didn't hear any movement, so she repeated the request. "I asked you to leave."

"I'm not going anywhere until you've heard what I have to say."

"You have nothing to say that I want to hear."

"Whether you want to or not, I'm going to tell you."

She didn't answer. Focusing her gaze on a painting of a field of flowers with a babbling brook running through it on the wall, she tried to tune him out as he related everything that had happened before she arrived. She was successful, until she heard his question. "Did you look at the date on that letter?"

She turned to face him. His eyes were filled with emotion, their dark depths boring into her soul. "What?"

He repeated it, and she shook her head.

"It was dated three weeks before I met you. I carried it around all that time because something stopped me from mailing it. That day at the train depot, I realized I couldn't ever mail it because she wasn't the woman I wanted."

Did she dare hope …? "She wasn't?"

"No." He leaned forward and rested his elbows on

the bed. Their eyes met, and his work-roughened hands covered hers. "I started falling in love with you that day and I've fallen more in love with you every day since."

Lynna heard his voice, but she barely heard anything after he said he loved her. "You love me?"

He nodded. "I do. I didn't know I could love anybody that much until I met you."

Gritting her teeth against the pain every movement caused, she tried to move closer to him.

"What are you doing?" Jasper got up and leaned over her. "You're going to hurt yourself even more. Grace said you need to rest in bed and heal. Nothing else."

She grinned through her pain. "Nothing?"

She wanted … no, she needed … to feel his arms around her and his lips on hers, to hear his heart beat against hers.

He paused, his face only inches from hers. "Lynna?"

"I love you, too," she said.

"You do? Then why are you so hell-bent on leaving?"

"I was leaving because I couldn't bear to see you with her, to know you loved her and not me."

He kissed her then, tenderly, with a promise of tomorrow. When he finally released her, she gazed up at him, wondering how her heart could hold such happiness. Her eyes stung with unshed tears. "And that proposal is still open?"

"It always will be until you say yes."

For a long moment, their gazes held, her thoughts drifting to the past and to the future.

She'd escaped marriage to a man she despised, and it had brought her to the man she'd love until she took her last breath. Fate. Destiny. God's will. Whatever it was, she'd be eternally grateful.

Finally, she smiled up at him, knowing without a doubt that this was where she was meant to be. "Yes."

The church bell pealed as Lynna's father drew the buggy to a stop in front of the church and helped her down.

Her father gazed at the small whitewashed building and let out a slight chuckle. "This church is a bit smaller than the one in Boston."

Lynna grinned. Rocky Ridge's only church wasn't the brick and stone cathedral-size church she'd attended in Boston, but in her eyes, it was big enough for the important people in her life, and that was what mattered.

She climbed the steps. At the top, she paused, adjusting her dress. No, it wasn't imported silk like the one she wore on her last wedding day, and the flowers weren't from the most prestigious florist in Boston, but she'd chosen them herself and were exactly what she'd wanted.

This was her wedding day, and it was perfect.

As she tucked her hand into her father's elbow and they made their way down the small aisle to where Jasper was waiting for her, she smiled at her family and the new friends she'd made – her mother, Mrs. Platt, Deirdre and her family, as well as many of the townspeople she'd come to know in the weeks since her accident. It seemed like everyone in town had come to share in their celebration.

"You look beautiful," Jasper whispered when she joined him at the front of the church. She flushed, her heart swelling with love for this man who'd given her everything she'd ever dreamed of. She adjusted the sleeve of her dress so that her fingers were free for him to place the plain gold band on her finger when the time came.

Tears spilled over when she recited her vows, and her heart overflowed with joy and love when she heard Jasper say his.

"You can kiss your bride now, Jasper," she heard the pastor say a few minutes later after he'd placed the ring on her finger.

Cupping her face in his hands, he kissed her, the kiss filled with promise of a future filled with love.

Soon after, they left the church and climbed into Jasper's buggy to go to the hotel where their wedding feast was being held.

When he helped her down a few minutes later, he wrapped his arms around her. "I thought I'd never be able to find a woman I could love the way my folks loved each other. I was lucky, even though it took a runaway bride to find it."

"I don't ever have to run again, except into your arms. I'm glad you waited for me."

He grinned and kissed her. "Me too."

ABOUT THE AUTHOR

Although she grew up far from the American west she writes about, Margery Scott has always been interested in stories about the men and women who settled the untamed land west of the Mississippi.

A transplanted Scot, Margery now lives in Canada with her husband. When she's not writing or traveling in search of the perfect setting for her next novel, you can usually find her wielding a pair of knitting needles or a pool cue.

Website: www.margeryscott.com
Email: margery@margeryscott.com
Newsletter: www.margeryscott.com/newsletter
VIP Facebook reader group: www.
facebook.com/groups/margeryscott

www.ingramcontent.com/pod-product-compliance
Lightning Source LLC
Chambersburg PA
CBHW030758200726
48288CB00004B/1233